"What are you trying to do, D...

"Ask you on a date," she said, her expression innocent. "Wasn't I clear enough?"

He studied her suspiciously. "What if I said I'd take you to some other pub in the city?"

"Then I'd say you're avoiding your brother," she responded. "And you certainly wouldn't want me to get an idea like that, would you?"

Sean held up his hands in a gesture of surrender. "We'll go the first weekend I'm off," he said.

To his surprise, instead of feeling trapped, he felt a faint stirring of genuine anticipation. Maybe it was Sean's turn to take a risk and keep the lines of communication open.

He met Deanna's penetrating gaze, saw the warm approval in her eyes and realized that there could be yet another benefit to taking a tiny chink out of the wall around his heart. Eventually there just might be enough room for a woman like Deanna to squeeze through.

Dear Reader,

I'm delighted to introduce Barbara Gale, whose intense story *The Ambassador's Vow* (SSE #1500) "explores not only issues involved in interracial romance, but the price one pays for not following one's heart." The author adds, "Together, the characters discover that honesty is more important to the heart than skin color. Recognizing the true worth of the gold ring they both sought is what eventually reunites them." Don't wait to pick this one up!

Sherryl Woods brings us *Sean's Reckoning* (SSE #1495), the next title in her exciting series THE DEVANEYS. Here, a firefighter discovers love and family with a single mom and her son when he rescues them from a fire. Next, a warning: there's another Bravo bachelor on the loose in Christine Rimmer's *Mercury Rising* (SSE #1496), from her miniseries THE SONS OF CAITLIN BRAVO. Perplexed heroine Jane Elliott tries to resist Cade Bravo, but of course her efforts are futile as she falls for the handsome hero. Did we ever doubt it?

In *Montana Lawman* (SSE #1497), part of MONTANA MAVERICKS, Allison Leigh makes the sparks fly between a shy librarian and a smitten deputy sheriff. Crystal Green's miniseries KANE'S CROSSING continues with *The Stranger She Married* (SSE #1498), in which a husband returns after a long absence—but he can't remember his marriage! Watch how this powerful love story unites this starry-eyed couple.... Finally, Tracy Sinclair delivers tantalizing excitement in *An American Princess* (SSE #1499), in which an American beauty receives royal pampering by a suave Prince Charming. How's that for a dream come true?

Each month, we aim to bring you the best in romance. We are enthusiastic to hear your thoughts. You may send comments to my attention at Silhouette Special Edition, 300 East 42nd Street, 6th Floor, New York, New York 10017. In the meantime, happy reading!

Sincerely,
Karen Taylor Richman
Senior Editor

Please address questions and book requests to:
Silhouette Reader Service
U.S.: 3010 Walden Ave., P.O. Box 1325, Buffalo, NY 14269
Canadian: P.O. Box 609, Fort Erie, Ont. L2A 5X3

SEAN'S RECKONING

SHERRYL WOODS

Silhouette®

SPECIAL EDITION™

Published by Silhouette Books

America's Publisher of Contemporary Romance

SILHOUETTE BOOKS

ISBN 0-373-24495-9

SEAN'S RECKONING

Copyright © 2002 by Sherryl Woods

Books by Sherryl Woods

Silhouette Special Edition

Silhouette Desire

Silhouette Books

*Vows
‡And Baby Makes Three
**The Bridal Path
††And Baby Makes Three:
   The Next Generation
◊And Baby Makes Three:
   The Delacourts of Texas
§The Calamity Janes
‡‡The Devaneys

SHERRYL WOODS

has written more than seventy-five novels. She also operates her own bookstore, Potomac Sunrise, in Colonial Beach, Virginia. If you can't visit Sherryl at her store, then be sure to drop her a note at P.O. Box 490326, Key Biscayne, FL 33149 or check out her Web site at www.sherrylwoods.com.

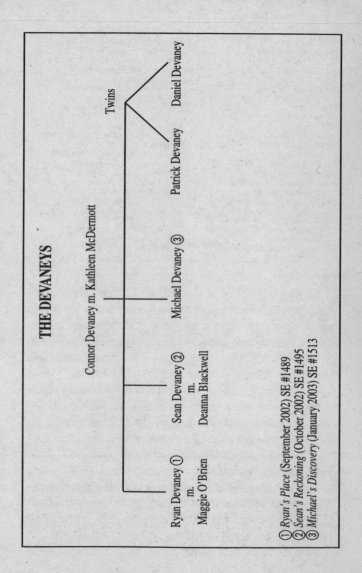

THE DEVANEYS

Connor Devaney m. Kathleen McDermott

Ryan Devaney ①
m.
Maggie O'Brien

Sean Devaney ②
m.
Deanna Blackwell

Michael Devaney ③

Twins

Patrick Devaney   Daniel Devaney

① *Ryan's Place* (September 2002) SE #1489
② *Sean's Reckoning* (October 2002) SE #1495
③ *Michael's Discovery* (January 2003) SE #1513

Chapter One

Sean Devaney's eyes were stinging from the smoke at the still-smoldering ruins of a tumbledown Victorian house that had been converted into low-rent apartments. Bits of ash clung to his sweat-dampened skin and hair. Even after stripping off his flame-retardant jacket and coveralls, Sean continued to feel as if he'd just exited an inferno...which he had. The acrid smell of smoke was thick in the air and in his clothes. Even after ten years with the Boston Fire Department, he still wasn't used to the aftermath of fighting a blaze—the exhaustion, the dehydration, the stench.

He'd been young and idealistic when he'd joined the department. He'd wanted to be a hero, craved the rush of adrenaline that kicked in when an alarm sounded. Saving lives had been part of it, but so had the danger, the thrill of putting his own life on the line to do something that mattered. In fact, it seemed Sean had spent most of his life trying to matter in one way or another.

Now, though, with the adrenaline wearing off, all he wanted was a warm, pounding shower and about sixteen straight hours of sleep. Unfortunately, until these last hot spots were thoroughly dampened and the location made secure, Sean was destined to stay right here just in case there was another flare-up.

The landlord was damn lucky no one had been killed. Indeed, from what Sean had observed inside, the landlord of this building himself ought to be shot. Even in the midst of battling heat and flames, Sean had noticed that there were so many code violations, he couldn't begin to count them all. Though it would be another twenty-four hours before investigators pinned down the cause of the blaze, in Sean's opinion it was most likely the outdated and overloaded electrical system. He hoped the landlord had a healthy insurance policy, because he was going to need it to pay off all the suits from his tenants. Most had lost just about everything to flames or to extensive smoke and water damage.

Sean scanned what remained of the crowd that had gathered to watch the inferno to see if there was any sign of a likely landlord, but most of the onlookers appeared to be more fascinated than dismayed by the destruction.

"Hey, Sean," his partner, Hank DiMartelli, called out, a grin splitting his face as he gestured toward something behind Sean. "Looks like we've got a new helper. He's agile enough, but I doubt he meets the department's age and height requirements."

Sean turned around just in time to catch a kid scrambling inside the fire truck. By the time Sean latched on to him, the boy was already reaching with unerring precision for the button to set off the siren.

"Whoa, fella, I think this neighborhood's heard enough sirens for one afternoon," Sean said, lifting the boy out of the truck.

"But I wanna do it," the child protested, chin jutting out in a mulish expression. With his light-brown hair standing up in gelled spikes, he looked a little like a pint-size member of one of those popular boy bands.

"Another time," Sean said very firmly. He set the boy on his feet on the ground and was surprised when the kid didn't immediately take off. Instead he stood there with his unrepentant expression and continued to cast surreptitious glances toward the cab of the engine. Sean had a hunch the boy would be right back up there unless Sean stuck close by to prevent it.

"So," he said, hoping to drag the boy's attention away from his fascination with the siren, "what's your name?"

The kid returned his gaze with a solemn expression. "I'm not supposed to tell it to strangers," he said automatically, as if the lesson had been drilled into him.

Sean hated to contradict such wise parental advice, but he also wanted to know to whom the kid belonged and why he was wandering around the scene of a fire all alone. "Normally I'd agree with that," he assured the boy. "But it's okay to tell me. I'm Sean, a fireman. Police officers and firefighters are good guys. You can always come to us when you're in trouble."

"But I'm not in trouble," he responded reasonably, his stubborn expression never wavering. "Besides, Mommy said never to tell *anyone* unless she said it was okay."

Sean bit back a sigh. He couldn't very well argue with that. "Okay then, where is your mom?"

The kid shrugged. "Don't know."

Sean's blood ran cold. Instantly he was six years old again, standing outside a school waiting for his mom after his first day of first grade. She had never come. In fact, that was the day she and Sean's father had disappeared from Boston and from his life. Soon afterward, he and two of his brothers were sent into foster care, separated forever. Only recently had Sean been found by his older brother, Ryan. To this day, he had no idea what had become of his younger brother, Michael, or of the twins, who'd apparently vanished with his parents.

Forcing himself back to the present, Sean looked into the boy's big brown eyes, searching for some sign of the sort of panic he'd experienced on that terrible day, but there was none. The kid looked perfectly comfortable with the fact that his mom was nowhere around.

Pushing aside his own knee-jerk reaction to the situation, he asked, "Where do you live?"

"I used to live there," the boy said matter-of-factly, pointing toward the scorched Victorian.

Dear God in heaven, was it possible that this child's mother was still inside? Had they missed her? Sean's thoughts scrambled. No way. They had searched every room methodically for any sign of victims of the fire that had started at midafternoon and raged for two hours before being brought under control. He'd gone through the two third-floor apartments himself. His partner had gone through the second floor. Another team had searched the first floor.

"Was your mom home when the fire started?" Sean

asked, keeping his tone mild. The last thing he wanted to do was scare the boy.

"Don't think so. I stay with Ruby when I get home from school. She lives over there." He pointed to a similar Victorian behind them. "Sometimes Mommy doesn't get home till really, really late. Then she takes me home and tucks me in, even if I'm already asleep."

The kid kept inadvertently pushing one of Sean's hot buttons. Another wave of anger washed through him. How could any mother leave a kid like this in the care of strangers while she cavorted around town half the night? What sort of irresponsible woman was she? If there was any one thing that could send Sean's usually placid temper skyrocketing, it was a negligent parent. He did his best to stay out of situations where he might run into one. The last time he'd worked a fire set by a kid playing with matches while his parents were out, he'd lost it. They'd had to drag Sean away from the boy's father when the man had finally shown up, swearing he'd only been away from the house for a few minutes. Sean had really wanted to beat some sense into him. A few minutes was a lifetime to a kid intent on mischief.

"Is Ruby around now?" Sean asked, managing to avoid giving any hint about his increasingly low opinion of the boy's mother. He even managed to keep his tone neutral.

The boy bobbed his head and pointed down the street. "Ruby doesn't have a phone, 'cause it costs too much. She went to the store on the corner to call Mom and tell her what happened. I went with her, but then I came back to see the truck."

Great! Just great, Sean thought. The baby-sitter had let the kid run off alone, too. He had half a mind to put in a call to Social Services on the spot. The only thing stopping him was his own lousy experience in the system. Plenty of kids were well served by foster care, but he hadn't been one of them, not until the last family had taken him in when he was almost ten.

The Forresters had been kind and patient and determined to prove to him that he was a kid worthy of being loved. They had almost made up for his having had his real parents walk out on him and two of his brothers. The Forresters had made up for some of the too-busy foster parents who hadn't had the time or the skills necessary to reassure a scared kid who was fearful that every adult in his life was going to leave and never come back. Foster care, by its very temporary nature, only fed that insecurity.

Since this child, despite wandering around on his own, showed no other apparent signs of neglect, Sean decided to check things out a bit more before taking a drastic step that could change the boy's life forever. He looked the kid in the eye. "So, how about I call you Mikey? I had a kid brother named Mike a long time ago. You remind me of him. He was pretty adventurous, too."

"That's not my name," the boy said.

Sean waited as the kid hesitated, clearly weighing parental cautions against current circumstances. He was probably trying to calculate the odds that Sean would let him back into that fire truck if they were on a first-name basis.

"You really don't think my mom would be mad if I told you my name?" he asked worriedly.

"I'm pretty sure she'd tell you it was okay, since I'm a firefighter," Sean reassured him. "You can at least tell me your first name."

The boy's brow knit as he considered that. "Okay," he said at last, his expression brightening. "I suppose it would be okay if you called me Seth."

Sean bit back a grin at the reluctant concession. "Okay then, Seth, why don't we sit right here on the curb and watch for Ruby to come back?"

Seth regarded him eagerly. "I could go get her. She'd probably want to meet you. Ruby's really beautiful and she's always looking for a new boyfriend. Are you married?"

"Nope, and I think it's best if we wait right here," Sean said, praying for protection from the too-available Ruby and her pint-size matchmaker. "So, Seth, you haven't told me about your dad. Is he at work?"

For the first time, the boy showed evidence of real dismay. His lower lip trembled. "I don't have a dad," he said sadly. "He went away a long, long time ago when I was just a baby. I'm almost six now. Well, not till next March. I know that's a long time from now, but being six is going to be really cool, 'cause I'll be in first grade."

Sean struggled to follow the conversation. He wasn't sure what to say to the announcement that the boy's father had abandoned him, but Seth didn't seem to notice. He kept right on chatting, spilling the details of his life.

"Mom says my dad loved me, but Ruby says he was a no-good son of a something. I'm not sure what." He regarded Sean with hopeful eyes. "Do you think Mom's right?"

Old emotions crowded in, and Sean bit back a string of curses. "I'm sure she is," he reassured the boy. "What dad wouldn't love a great kid like you?"

"Then how come he went away?" Seth asked reasonably.

"I don't know," Sean told him with total honesty. It certainly wasn't something he could understand. Not in Seth's case, not in his own, even with an adult's perspective on it. He told Seth the same thing he'd been told on countless occasions. "Sometimes things happen that can't be helped. And sometimes we never find out why."

Sean sighed. He certainly hadn't. And until Ryan had come back into his life, he had told himself he didn't care. In fact, he'd gone out of his way not to be found, in case his folks had ever gotten around to looking. He'd stayed in Boston, but he'd maintained a deliberately low profile—an unlisted phone number, no credit cards. Anyone looking for him would have had to work hard to find him. That way, when no one had come knocking at his door, he'd been able to tell himself it was because he'd been all but impossible to find. He'd never had to deal with the possibility that no one had cared enough to look.

His brother Ryan had apparently erected the same sort of walls around his heart. Then he'd fallen in love with Maggie, who had prodded him into searching for the family he'd lost. Sean's safeguards hadn't been enough to stop a determined investigator from finding him, which told Sean that his parents had more than likely never bothered to try. Most of the time he could convince himself that that didn't hurt, but there were times like this when the wounds felt as raw as they had more than twenty years ago.

Just when he was about to sink into a disgusting bout of self-pity, a dark-haired woman wearing a waitress's uniform came racing down the street, her ex-

pression frantic. She was trailed by a sexy blonde
wearing tight jeans, a bright pink tank top and spike
heels.

"Mom," Seth shouted, leaping up and racing
straight for the petite, dark-haired woman.

She scooped him up, smothered his face in kisses,
then held him out to examine him from head to toe.
Only then did she speak. "What are you doing back
here, young man?" she demanded, her expression
stern. "You know you're never supposed to go anywhere unless Ruby's with you."

"I came to see the fire truck," he said, then pointed
accusingly at Sean, who'd risen to join them. "He
wouldn't let me play with the siren, though."

The woman turned toward Sean and held out a
hand. "I'm Deanna Blackwell. Thanks for keeping an
eye on him. I hope he wasn't any bother."

"Sean Devaney," he said tightly. Looking into
huge brown eyes filled with sincerity, Sean couldn't
bring himself to deliver the lecture that had been form-
ing in his head from the moment he'd run across the
kid. Before he could say anything at all, the second
woman stepped forward and slid a hand provocatively
up his arm. The muscle tensed at her touch, but beyond that he was pretty much immune to the invitation
in her eyes.

"I'm Ruby Allen, the baby-sitter," she said, regarding him seductively. "I've always wanted to meet
a real, honest-to-goodness firefighter."

Deanna rolled her eyes at the provocative come-on.
"You'll have to excuse Ruby," she apologized.
"She's basically harmless."

A lot of men would fall for Ruby's sex-on-the-run
attitude, but Sean wasn't even tempted. His dates

tended to be smart, independent types who weren't looking for a future. Ruby had desperation written all over her. She might act as if she were looking for nothing more than a roll in the hay, but instinct—and Seth's innocent remark—suggested otherwise.

Deanna Blackwell was another story entirely. With her fragile features and huge eyes emphasized by dark curls that had been cropped very short in a no-muss, no-fuss style, she looked about as innocent as her kid. The stay-out-all-night playgirl mom he'd been anticipating was, instead, an angel with smudges of exhaustion under her eyes. *That* was a combination that could get under his skin. That was one reason he avoided the type at all costs.

At the sound of a shout across the street, Deanna suddenly turned toward the house that had apparently been her home. The relief at having found her son gave way to a shock so profound, her knees buckled.

Sean caught her before she fell, inhaling a faint whiff of some soft, feminine perfume that made his pulse leap. The skin of her arms was soft and smooth as satin against his rough palms. When he gazed into her eyes, they were filled with tears and a level of dismay that almost broke his heart. No matter how many times he saw people hit between the eyes by that sudden recognition of everything they'd lost, he'd never been able to steel himself against their pain.

"I'm sorry," he said, reaching for a fresh bottle of water inside the truck and holding it out for her. "Sit down for a minute and drink this."

She sank onto the fire truck's running board. "I had no idea," she whispered, looking from him to Ruby and back again. "I thought...I don't know what I thought, but it wasn't this. What am I going to do?

We didn't have much to begin with, but everything we owned was in there."

Sean exchanged a look with Ruby, whose helpless expression encouraged him to take over and reply.

"But you and Seth are safe," he said, dredging up a familiar platitude. It was a reminder he'd delivered a hundred times, but he knew it was small comfort to someone who'd seen everything they owned—all the sentimental keepsakes from the past—go up in flames. There was always a gut-wrenching sense of loss even when they understood that life was more important than property.

He held her gaze. "You know that's what really matters, don't you?"

"Yes, of course, but—" She shook her head as if something had confused her. "You said something about Seth?"

"Your boy."

She turned to the child in question, an unexpected grin suddenly tugging at her lips. "Why did you tell him your name is Seth?"

"Because I'm never supposed to tell my name to strangers," he said dutifully. He slid a guilty look toward Sean. "I'm sorry I lied."

Sean was surprised at having been taken in by a pint-size con artist. "You're not Seth?"

The kid shook his head.

"Then who's Seth?"

"He's my friend at school," the boy admitted. "I wanted to do what Mom said, but I figured you had to call me something if we were gonna be friends."

"At least one lesson stuck," Deanna Blackwell said gratefully, then met Sean's gaze. "His name is Kevin.

I hope you won't hold this against him. He was trying to do the right thing.''

Sean chuckled at the clever deception. He'd deserved it for pushing so hard. Maybe she was doing a better job with the kid than he'd been giving her credit for. Maybe she was just a struggling single mom doing the best she could.

"No problem," he reassured both of them. "Look, if you need a temporary place to stay, there are services available that can help. I can make a call to the Red Cross for you. Your insurance will kick in in a few days."

She shook her head. "No insurance."

He should have guessed, given the sorry state of the building even before the fire. Anyone forced to live here probably couldn't afford insurance. "The landlord probably has some," he suggested.

"On the building, not the contents," she said. "He made that very clear when we moved in."

"Even so, if he's found liable through some kind of negligence, he can be sued."

"You're assuming I could afford a lawyer to handle the suit," she said despondently. "I know what they charge, and I couldn't even afford an hour of their time."

Sean desperately wanted to find something that would put some life back into her eyes. "What about your family? Can they help?"

She shook her head, her expression grim. "That's not possible," she said tightly. "Look, this isn't your problem. You've done more than enough just by keeping Kevin out of mischief, when there are probably far more important things you ought to be doing. We'll manage."

"Stop worrying, Dee. You two can stay with me," Ruby volunteered, giving Deanna Blackwell a reassuring hug. "It'll be crowded, but we can make it work. You're hardly ever home, anyway, and Kevin's already with me every afternoon. I can loan you some clothes, too."

Sean tried to imagine Deanna wearing Ruby's tight-fitting clothes, but the image wouldn't come. Impulsively he reached for his wallet and peeled off a hundred dollars and tucked it into her hand. Before Deanna could protest, he said, "It's a loan, not charity. You can pay me when you get back on your feet."

He saw pride warring with practicality, but then she glanced down at Kevin. That seemed to stiffen her resolve. She faced Sean. "Thank you. I will pay you back."

"I'm not worried about it," he told her.

"But I always pay my debts. It's important to me. Where can I find you?"

"At the fire station three blocks over most of the time," he said, though he was mentally kissing that money goodbye. Years ago he'd learned the lesson never to lend anything if he couldn't afford to lose it. He'd taken very few possessions with him when he'd left home, and since then he hadn't bothered to accumulate much that had any sentimental value. As for money, it was nice to have, but he wasn't obsessed with it. And he had few material needs that couldn't be met with his next paycheck.

"Bring my pal Kevin by sometime, and I'll let him try out the siren," he suggested, giving the boy a solemn wink.

"All right!" Kevin said.

Satisfied at last that Kevin was in better hands than

he'd originally assumed, Sean jogged back across the street to check on the progress being made at the fire. Only an occasional wisp of smoke rose from the ashes. They'd be out of here soon and he'd be off in a couple of hours. Sleep beckoned like a sultry mistress.

"Way to go, Sean!" Hank said, enthusiastically slapping him on the back. "I saw you with the only two females under the age of seventy in this entire neighborhood. Did you get the number of the hot blonde?"

"Like I really wanted it," Sean scoffed. "She's your type, not mine."

Hank regarded him with disappointment. "How about the brunette with the kid?"

"Nope."

"Two gorgeous women and you struck out completely?" Hank asked incredulously. "Man, you *are* slipping."

"I didn't strike out," Sean told him patiently. "I never even got in the game."

"Why the hell not?"

Sean wondered about that himself. Maybe it was because one woman was definitely not his type and because the other one struck him as being just a little too needy and vulnerable, despite that streak of stubborn pride. It was one thing to rescue someone who'd just lost her home. It was quite another to allow himself to get emotionally entangled. He always tried to keep his protective instincts on a short leash.

Hank sidled up to him and held out a metal toy fire truck. "It's not too late," he consoled Sean. "This probably belonged to the kid. Hang on to it. Unless you're a whole lot dumber than I think you are, something tells me one of these days you're going to be looking for an excuse to see his mom again.''

''No way,'' Sean said fiercely.

But even as he uttered the denial, he took the truck and tucked it into his pocket. He told himself it was a reflexive gesture simply to keep it out of Hank's hands, but the truth was, his partner had him pegged. Despite all the alarm bells in his head, Deanna Blackwell's vulnerability tugged at him like an invisible rope.

He glanced back toward the spot where she'd been standing, but she was gone. He was surprised by the intensity of his disappointment.

Then he caught a glimpse of the flashy blonde disappearing into a building across the street, and something akin to relief spread through him. If—and that was a really huge *if*—he ever lost his mind and decided he wanted to see Deanna Blackwell again, Ruby would know where to find her.

He grinned as he considered whether Ruby would be inclined to give up that information, or whether, like Kevin, she'd choose to be tight-lipped. Only one thing to do if that happened, he concluded. He'd introduce her to Hank, who could wheedle information out of any female on earth.

Now there, he thought with a chuckle, was a match made in heaven. Maybe one day when he was really bored, he'd get the two of them hooked up together just to watch the sparks fly. And if he ran into Deanna Blackwell in the process...well, that would just be an accidental act of fate.

Chapter Two

"That man was so into you," Ruby teased Deanna as they climbed the steps to Ruby's third-floor apartment, which was going to be home for who knew how long.

"He was not," Deanna said, grateful for the teasing because it was, temporarily at least, keeping her mind off the fire and her uncertain future. "No man ever looks at me twice when you're around."

"This one did," Ruby insisted, leading the way into her one-bedroom apartment with its tiny kitchen and a bathroom no bigger than a closet, which it probably had been before the house had been converted to apartments. She grinned at Deanna. "And you've got something I don't have."

It was hard to imagine anything that the sexy, self-confident Ruby didn't possess, especially when it came to the sort of attributes that appealed to men.

Sadly, far too few of them took the time to look beneath Ruby's flashy looks and impressive chest. It infuriated Deanna that they never saw the kind, generous woman who would do anything in the world for a friend, something she was proving right now by inviting Deanna and Kevin to stay with her.

Deanna regarded Ruby with curiosity. "What on earth could I have that you don't?"

Ruby ducked her head into the refrigerator so that her reply was muffled, but Deanna had no trouble hearing her.

"Kevin," she said. She stood up, held out a soda and met Deanna's gaze. "I watched the two of them together out there. Fireman Sean is definitely daddy material. Something to think about, don't you agree?"

Deanna sighed and accepted the soft drink. "Ruby, we've been over this a million times. Unlike you, I am not looking for a man to make my life complete."

Ruby scowled at her. "Not complete, just easier."

"I can take care of myself and Kevin," Deanna insisted.

"When it comes to being a loving, wonderful mom, you're the best," Ruby agreed. "But the way I see it, Kevin could sure use a daddy to replace that scumbag who left the two of you. Not that I don't think you're better off without Frankie, but he has left a huge hole in Kevin's life. Even you have to see that. The kid asks a million and one questions about his dad on a daily basis. That one snapshot he has of Frankie is practically worn bare from his constant handling."

"I know," Deanna admitted. If she hadn't seen it for herself, she had Ruby to point it out with disgusting frequency.

"Well then, don't you owe it to Kevin to take another look at fireman Sean?"

"I'm not getting involved with some guy just so my son has a father figure in his life," Deanna said impatiently. "Besides, he has Joey."

Ruby nearly choked on her soft drink as she let out a hoot of laughter. "You want Joey Talifero to be your son's role model? Are you nuts?"

"There's nothing wrong with Joey." Deanna reacted defensively as she always did when Ruby said something disparaging about her boss. "He's a perfectly respectable businessman."

"I'll give you respectable, if by that you mean he probably hasn't deliberately broken any laws lately. But he has a tenth-grade education, if that. He owns a two-bit restaurant and spends all his spare time betting on the ponies," Ruby countered.

"He has a heart of gold, and he and Pauline treat me like family," Deanna retorted.

"If you mean Joey overworks you and underpays you, I agree," Ruby replied. "And I notice you didn't mention your other boss as having hero potential."

Deanna and Ruby both worked at a small law firm in the neighborhood, Deanna as a full-time receptionist, Ruby as a part-time clerk. Their boss, Jordan Hodges, was not the kind of man who invited a lot of personal chitchat on the job. He was all business. Deanna wasn't even entirely sure he was aware she had a son, and she did her best to make sure that Kevin didn't interfere with her job performance. She needed that minimal salary and her tips from working at Joey's in the evenings just to scrape by.

"Mr. Hodges would be a great role model," she

said stiffly, "assuming he was the least bit interested in being one."

"Yeah, right," Ruby scoffed. "Come on, Dee. Think about it. Don't you think a friendly fireman would be a better choice in the hero department than either Joey or stiff-necked Hodges?"

Deanna thought about the man who'd befriended her son that afternoon. Goodness knows, even covered with soot and sweat, he'd been the most handsome male she'd run across in years. Coal-black hair, blue eyes, square jaw, well-defined muscles. Definitely the stuff of fantasies. He'd been kind to Kevin. He'd even loaned her money. Beyond that, though, she knew absolutely nothing about him. How much could you really tell about a man's character in a twenty-minute encounter? She'd known Frankie Blackwell for a year before she'd married him, and look how that had turned out. Better the devil she knew—Joey, or even Jordan Hodges—than the one she didn't.

Besides, Joey would never in a million years hit on her. His wife would strangle him. Deanna wasn't so sure about this Sean Devaney. If what Ruby said about the way he'd looked at her was true—and Ruby definitely had reliable instincts where men were concerned—how long would it be before he wanted more from her than she was interested in giving? And how long after that before she made the second-worst mistake of her life by starting to count on him, just as she had once foolishly counted on Frankie Blackwell? Nope, the status quo was definitely safer. Since Frankie had walked out on her and their son, she'd learned to rely on no one except herself. Ruby was the one exception.

Studying her friend's tight jeans and stretched-to-the-limits tank top, Deanna understood why people got the wrong idea about Ruby. But Deanna knew better. She would trust Ruby with her life. She did trust her with Kevin's safety almost every single afternoon and evening. Ruby had never let her down. Deanna counted herself blessed to have such a friend in her life.

"I have more pressing things to worry about than a role model for Kevin," she said, dismissing the entire uncomfortable topic. "In case it's slipped your mind, I've lost my home and everything I own."

Suddenly the enormity of that had her knees buckling for the second time that day. This time there was no strong firefighter there to keep her from collapsing. Instead, she sank onto the sofa, blinking back the hot sting of tears.

"Ruby, what am I going to do?" she asked, relieved that Kevin had stopped off downstairs to play with a friend. He clearly didn't understand just how dire things were, and she didn't want him to witness her distress. There were more than enough uncertainties in his life as it was, things she had no more control over than she did the rise and fall of the moon each day.

"You're going to do exactly what you always do," Ruby said with complete confidence. "You're going to draw on that unlimited reserve of strength that has gotten you through in the past, and I'm going to do everything I can to help you. We'll manage. That's what friends do in a crisis. You were there for me when my world crashed down around me. Now it's my turn to return the favor."

Ruby's reassuring words barely registered. Deanna was mentally calculating dollars and cents for the bare necessities. Even with Sean's hundred dollars in her pocket and a tiny bit of savings in the bank, she was going to come up short. Way short. She sighed wearily.

"I was barely making it as it was. How can I find a new place, pay a security deposit, furnish it and buy all new stuff for Kevin and me?" she asked, overwhelmed by the task ahead of her. "We don't even have a toothbrush."

"Stop worrying. Kevin has a toothbrush here. He also has clothes and toys here," Ruby reminded her. "And you wear those blah uniforms at Joey's. At least one's got to be at the laundry, right? You can pick up a couple of skirts for your job at the law firm with that cash Sean loaned you. And my blouses will fit you. You can borrow anything in the closet. As for finding a place to stay, we've already discussed that. You'll stay right here."

"For a night or two, maybe, but you can't have us underfoot indefinitely."

"Why can't I?" Ruby asked indignantly.

"For one thing, you only have one bedroom."

"So? We can share it, and Kevin can sleep on the sofa," Ruby insisted, determinedly putting the best possible spin on the situation. "He's been falling asleep there on the nights you work late, anyway."

"I'm grateful for the offer, I really am, but won't that play havoc with your social life?"

Ruby shot her a wry look. "It's not like it's all that hot at the moment, anyway. An excuse for a break will do me good. I can use the time to reevaluate the way I'm going about choosing the men I date. Clearly I'm doing it all wrong."

Ruby sounded totally sincere, but Deanna studied her worriedly. "Are you sure? Really sure?"

"This is what friends do in a crisis," Ruby repeated. "Now quit worrying about it. We're going to be fine."

"I don't know how to thank—"

"No thanks are necessary, and if you keep it up, I'm going to get cranky. Now, I just got paid for helping Mrs. Carlyle clean her apartment, so I recommend we get Kevin and go out for pizza."

Deanna shook her head, struggling to her feet. "I have to get back to work."

"You most certainly do not. Joey knows what happened. I explained when I called. And I've already told him you won't be back in until at least tomorrow, possibly the day after."

"This is no time for me to miss work," Deanna protested, as panic rose up in her belly. "He could fire me."

Ruby grabbed her shoulders and shook her gently. "Hey, wake up. Not even Joey is dumb enough or mean enough to fire you under these circumstances. You're half the reason people keep coming back there. It's certainly not for his gourmet cooking. Now listen to me. You've just been through a trauma. In my experience the only thing to do in this kind of situation is eat comfort food. In fact, I think we ought to follow the pizza with hot-fudge sundaes."

Despite her dismay over the wild spin her life was taking, Deanna laughed. "I'm the one with the crisis. How come you get to indulge?"

"I'm giving up men." Ruby winked at her. "In my book, *that* is a genuine trauma."

For Deanna, who'd given up on men after being dumped by Kevin's dad, it didn't seem like any sacrifice at all, but she wasn't Ruby. Ruby might have been devastated by her divorce, but she'd bounced right back into the game. She made no apologies at all for the fact that she enjoyed having a man in her life.

"You could always take Kevin to the fire station. Try your luck with Sean Devaney again," Deanna suggested, ignoring the surprising pang of dismay that swept through her at the prospect of pushing Ruby and Sean together.

"And have that gorgeous hunk reject me twice? I don't think so. A woman has to have some pride." Ruby regarded Deanna slyly. "Of course, when *you* take Kevin over there, I might just tag along and see what the rest of the pickings are like."

Deanna sighed heavily. "I suppose that's how I'm going to pay you back for taking me in."

"Absolutely."

An image of Sean Devaney crept into her head. The man *was* seriously gorgeous. What healthy woman wouldn't want to sneak another look at him? It didn't mean she was actually interested in anything more. And she did owe Ruby big-time.

"Done," she agreed eventually.

And based on the way her hormones dipped and swayed in jubilation even as she uttered the word, she'd better make very sure that all of her carefully honed defenses were firmly in place.

"And Mom said I shouldn't bother you because you're probably really busy, but I was thinking that if you weren't busy, maybe you could come over in the fire truck and take me for a ride," Kevin Blackwell was saying earnestly to Sean.

The call had come in on the nonemergency line at

the fire station about five minutes earlier. Sean had barely gotten a word in edgewise. The kid definitely had a lot to say, and he was saying it all in such a rush that Sean could barely keep up with him.

"Hey, Kevin, slow down, okay?" he said, laughing.

"Oh, okay. I thought you might be in a hurry."

"Not right this second," Sean reassured him. "How did you know how to find me?"

"It was easy. Ruby found the number in the phone book."

Ah, so the notorious Ruby was promoting this idea. For whose benefit? Sean wondered. The kid's or her own? Or was she by any chance matchmaking? That possibility intrigued him far more than it should.

"Is she there now?" Sean asked, hoping to clarify things before he agreed to anything.

"Uh-uh. I'm at the pay phone outside the laundry. Ruby's inside. She'll be out in a minute, though. She said it was okay if I called. It is, isn't it? You're not mad, are you?" he asked worriedly.

"No. I'm not mad. I'm glad to hear from you," Sean said, realizing it was true. He'd thought about the boy—and his mother—a lot the past couple of weeks. He'd dismissed the thoughts as perfectly normal under the circumstances. He often worried about people whose homes had been destroyed, though few of them haunted his dreams the way Deanna Blackwell had.

"How are you and your mom doing?" he asked.

"Okay, I guess. Staying with Ruby is kind of cool," Kevin said. "She keeps way better stuff in the refrigerator than Mom did."

Sean bit back a chuckle at the boy's standards. "Such as?"

"Ice cream and sodas and a whole bag of candy. Mom says I'm not supposed to touch that 'cause it's Ruby's crisis food, whatever that is. But I don't think she'd mind if I ate one candy bar, do you?"

"No, I don't imagine she would, as long as you asked permission first." More curious than he cared to admit, Sean asked, "Does Ruby have a lot of crises?" And what kind were they? he wondered. The kind no five-year-old should know about?

"I don't know," Kevin told him. "Maybe you could ask her. She just came out."

"In a minute," he said, hoping to put off a conversation with Ruby until he had plenty of backup to distract her, namely Hank. "I can't get away from here, but maybe you and Ruby can come on over to see the fire truck, like I promised."

"Wow, that would be cool," Kevin said enthusiastically. "You talk to her, okay? She'll do it if you ask. Here."

Sean heard the flurry of excited conversation on the other end, then finally Ruby took the phone.

"You sure know how to win a kid's heart," she said.

Sean ignored the compliment. "What about it? Can you bring him by?"

To his surprise she hesitated. "How about in a couple of hours? Will you be around after seven?"

"Never can tell when we'll get a call, but I imagine we will be. Any particular reason you want to wait?"

"Deanna will be home then. I know she wants to come along. I think she has some money she wants to pay you."

"I told her that there was no rush on that," he said, feeling unreasonably irritated that Deanna was in such a hurry to pay him back. Since he never liked being indebted to anyone himself, he realized he should be more understanding, but it rankled nonetheless. "It's only been a couple of weeks. She can't possibly be on her feet financially already."

"She isn't, but you don't know her," Ruby said, sounding every bit as exasperated as Sean felt. "She's got this mile-wide stubborn streak and more pride than any woman ought to have. She won't rest until she's paid you back every cent." She lowered her voice and confided, "Frankly, I think she's on the verge of collapse from exhaustion. She was already working two jobs. Ever since the fire, she's added extra hours at the restaurant. Tonight's her first night off, and she wouldn't have taken that if I hadn't called and told Joey he had to insist on it."

"You called her boss?" Sean asked, not sure whether to be impressed or shocked. "What did you do? Did you have to blackmail him?"

"Pretty much," she said cheerfully. "I told him if he didn't let her out of there, I'd come over and tell his customers he was a total creep for making her work all these extra hours when she's practically asleep on her feet." She paused. "And I might have mentioned something about spreading the word about a case of food poisoning I had recently."

Sean grinned at the thought of a vengeful Ruby descending on the hapless Joey. Whoever the poor man was, it was unlikely he would be a match for her.

"What about Kevin?" he asked. "Does Deanna have any time for him these days?"

"Kevin's okay. He's with me," she said, her voice immediately taking on a defensive edge, as if she understood the implied criticism of her friend.

"A boy needs his mom," Sean said fiercely, perfectly willing to risk Ruby's wrath to make his own point.

"Yeah, well, he needs a roof over his head, too," she retorted, switching gears to take her friend's side. "And Deanna's determined to give him that. I keep telling her she doesn't have to make it happen tomorrow, but she won't hear it." She hesitated, then added thoughtfully, "Maybe you can get through to her."

"Damn right I will," Sean muttered.

"What?"

"Nothing. But if you all come by, I'll talk to her."

"We'll see you in a couple of hours, then," Ruby said with what sounded like a hint of satisfaction in her voice.

Listening to her, Sean felt his gut tighten. He had his answer for sure now. The woman was matchmaking, no question about it. If he had half a brain in his head, he'd develop a sudden case of the flu and be long gone before they got to the station.

But an image of Kevin Blackwell's excited expression as he'd crawled up into that fire truck crept into Sean's head. Add to that the boy's obvious yearning for a man he could look up to, and Sean knew he wasn't going anywhere. There were plenty of men in the world who didn't think twice about disappointing a kid, whether their own or someone else's, but Sean would never be one of them. He'd lived with way too many disappointments of his own.

Deanna was still irritated by the way Joey had summarily dismissed her just as the dinner hour was getting into full swing. No matter how hard she'd argued that she needed the tips, he'd kept right on shooing her toward the door.

"Wednesdays are always slow," he'd said, despite the fact that every table was occupied. "How much would you make tonight, anyway?"

"Every little bit helps," Deanna had countered.

He'd opened the register, pulled out a twenty and slapped it into her hand. "This will make up for some of it, then. You need some sleep. You need to spend some time with your boy."

Deanna's gaze had narrowed at that. "You've been talking to Ruby, haven't you?"

"Ruby who?" he'd inquired with completely phony innocence.

"You know perfectly well who I'm talking about," she'd responded. Joey and Ruby had taken an almost instant dislike to each other years ago. They tried not to let it show in front of Deanna, but it was hard to miss. "Okay, if you and Ruby have actually reached an agreement about something, I know better than to argue with you. I'll go home. I'll spend some time with Kevin. I'll sleep."

Joey gave a nod of satisfaction. "And tomorrow you'll be back with a smile on your face for all the customers, so they'll double their usual tips."

"If only," Deanna had muttered. Most of Joey's customers were senior citizens living on fixed incomes. That was one reason they came for Joey's early-bird specials in the first place.

Now that she was actually on her way home, Deanna found her feet dragging. Exhaustion clawed at her. She would give just about anything for an hour in the tub, a glass of iced tea and twelve uninterrupted hours of sleep.

Instead she found Ruby and Kevin waiting for her on the front steps.

"You've got five minutes to go inside and make yourself beautiful," Ruby announced.

"Why?"

Kevin bounced up and down in front of her. "We're going to the fire station to see Sean. He invited us, didn't he, Ruby?"

Instantly suspicious, Deanna glanced at her friend. "Sean called?"

"Well, the truth is that Kevin called him, but Sean did ask us to come by. I spoke to him myself."

Deanna sensed a plot, one she wanted no part of. "Then why don't the two of you go on over there? You don't need me. You can take that cash I have for him."

Kevin's face fell. "But we waited for you, Mom. You've got to come."

"That's right," Ruby agreed, giving Kevin's hand a squeeze. "Sean's expecting all of us. You don't want to disappoint him, do you?" She glanced pointedly at Kevin to indicate that Sean wasn't the only one who was going to be disappointed if Deanna refused to go.

Pushing aside her exhaustion and her suspicions, Deanna forced a smile. "Okay then. Give me ten minutes to shower and change."

Kevin's expression promptly brightened. "Hurry, Mom. We don't want to keep him waiting too long. He might get too busy to see us. Or he might go home."

Deanna pressed a kiss to her son's forehead. "I'll hurry," she promised.

As she passed Ruby on her way up the steps, she

leaned down and whispered, "And I'll get even with you for this."

Ruby chuckled. "I doubt it. In fact, if things go the way I'm anticipating, someday you'll thank me. I left my red halter top on the bed. I think it's just the thing for you to wear on a hot night like this."

"Don't count on it."

"Mom!" Kevin whined.

"I'm going," she said, slipping inside and trudging up the stairs. Going to the fire station was absolutely the last thing she wanted to do tonight.

Unfortunately, she couldn't say quite the same thing about seeing Sean Devaney…and that reaction scared her to death.

Chapter Three

Sean tried to pretend that he wasn't watching for Deanna's arrival at the firehouse. He kept his nose buried in a book. As a kid he hadn't been much of a reader, but during the endless hours between calls at the station, he'd picked up a fantasy novel one of the other firefighters had just finished and he'd been hooked. He'd enjoyed the pure escape from reality into realms where good always triumphed over evil.

He was currently finishing up the latest Harry Potter book, enjoying the way the beleaguered kid stood up to the bullies around him. He couldn't help wishing he'd had Harry as a role model when he'd been a kid. Tonight, however, even though he was as engrossed in the latest adventure as he had been in all the others, his attention kept drifting to the sidewalk outside.

"Looking for anyone in particular?" Hank inquired, dropping into a chair next to him.

"Who says I'm looking for anyone?" Sean replied, testy at having been caught.

"Usually when you get lost in one of those books of yours, this place could burn down around you and you wouldn't notice, but tonight you seem distracted. You keep glancing toward the street."

Sean considered lying, but since he was going to need Hank's help to get some alone time with Deanna, he decided to come clean. "Deanna Blackwell's on her way over with her kid."

A grin spread across Hank's face. "I knew it!" he said triumphantly. "She's the doll from that fire a couple of weeks back, right? You've been seeing her all along on the sly, haven't you, you sneaky dog? I knew you were lying through your teeth when you claimed you weren't interested."

Sean frowned at him. "I have not been seeing her. The kid called today and wanted to come by to see the fire trucks. I said okay. It's no big deal."

"It's worth fifty bucks to me," Hank gloated.

Sean studied his friend's expression, looking for even the tiniest hint of guilt. "You actually had bets going on whether I'd see her again, didn't you?" he asked. Hank didn't even flinch.

"Well, of course I did," Hank said with no evidence of remorse. "Your love life—or lack thereof— is the subject of much speculation around here. All the guys keep wondering why you're not married, since every woman you meet falls madly in love with you."

"I don't see anyone long enough for them to fall in love with me," Sean contradicted.

"Which I explained to the guys, but they think you're just holding out on us, that you've got some gorgeous babe stashed away and that you sneak off to spend every spare minute making passionate love to her.''

Sean groaned. "You all clearly have too much time on your hands."

Hank grinned. "True enough. So, is the delectable Deanna bringing her hot friend with her?"

"If you're referring to Ruby, the answer's yes."

"Then I am forever in your debt," Hank said solemnly. "I have had a few incredibly steamy dreams about that woman."

"You have steamy dreams about every woman you pass on the street," Sean pointed out.

"This is different," Hank insisted.

Sean rolled his eyes at the familiar refrain. "I doubt that, but you can do me a favor. I need a few minutes alone with Deanna. Can I count on you to show Ruby and Kevin around?"

"When have you not been able to count on me?" Hank demanded indignantly. "No matter how trying the task, do I not step up to the plate when you ask?"

Sean chuckled. "Then I take it the answer is yes, even though this is one of those *trying* occasions?"

"Yes," Hank said, then added with exaggerated politeness, "And thank you for thinking of me. Those of us in the Boston Fire Department are here to serve and protect in whatever way we're called upon to do so."

"Try to remember that when you're thinking about hitting on Ruby," Sean cautioned, thinking of the way she'd neatly blackmailed Deanna's boss. "Something tells me she could bring you to your knees if you get out of line."

Hank made a show of swooning ecstatically. "This just keeps getting better and better. You know how I love a challenge."

"Don't make me regret this," Sean said.

"Have I ever let you down?"

Ah, Sean thought, that was the thing. For all of his fooling around and his penchant for chasing anything in skirts ever since his divorce, Hank DiMartelli was the best buddy a man could have. There was no one in the department Sean would rather have at his side going into a raging inferno. Hank was fearless and loyal and smart. He'd won more citations for bravery than anyone else at the station, Sean included.

Sean punched him in the arm. "Never," he agreed. "But there's a first time for everything, and in your case this better not be it."

Hank's gaze narrowed and his expression turned serious. "Why all the paternal concern for a woman you barely know and aren't interested in?"

Sean wasn't precisely sure himself. "She's Deanna's friend," he said, which was the closest he could come to summing it up. "And something tells me Deanna would be royally ticked if she thought I was throwing Ruby to the wolves, or to one wolf in particular. People seldom spot your finer qualities through all the bull."

"Then by all means, I'll be on my best behavior," Hank assured him. "I won't even try to cop a feel of those gorgeous breasts of hers."

Sean grinned at the concession despite himself. "Something tells me that's the last thing I need to worry about. I'm pretty sure Ruby can handle someone with roving hands. She's probably had a lot of practice. Maybe you should consider getting to know her for her mind."

"That body, and she has a mind, too?" Hank asked, his expression incredulous.

Sean scowled at his joking. "Go to hell."

Hank laughed. "But if I do, who'll show Miss Ruby and the kid around and get them out of your hair so you can practice seducing the lovely Deanna?"

"It's not about seduction, and I'm sure I can manage on my own, if it comes to that," Sean said. "In fact, showing them all around myself might be the smarter way to go."

"Forget it. Ruby's mine. You can have the single mom with the vulnerable look in her eyes. Just one question, though. I thought that was the type you tended to avoid like the plague. So what's up with this Deanna? How did she get under your skin?"

Sean sighed, not even bothering to deny Hank's claim that Deanna had gotten to him. "I wish I knew."

The walk to the fire station a few blocks from the apartment hadn't taken nearly as long as Deanna would have liked. She'd wanted to postpone this encounter with Sean Devaney for as long as possible, but with Kevin running ahead and demanding that she and Ruby hurry, they'd made it to the station in record time.

All the way over she had tried to prepare herself for the physical impact the sexy firefighter was likely to have on her again. She told herself that appreciating a man's body wasn't a crime, that it certainly wasn't anything that required some sort of commitment. She even consoled herself that her stomach probably wouldn't even flutter when she saw him again. It had probably been a one-time thing brought on by her overwrought condition on the day of the fire. Maybe he was really a toad.

But when Sean walked into view in his snug jeans and tight T-shirt, looking like a walking advertisement for testosterone, that weak-kneed effect slammed into her again. Deanna was forced to face the possibility that it hadn't been seeing the burned-out wreckage of her home that had drawn all the air out of her lungs that day. Maybe she'd just been subconsciously looking for an excuse to fall into this man's powerful arms.

Beside her, Ruby sucked in a breath. "My God, he's every bit as gorgeous as I remembered," she said in a stage whisper that Sean could easily hear.

"Stop it," Deanna whispered, her cheeks flaming. "You're embarrassing me."

"A work of art that impressive is meant to be appreciated," Ruby retorted with a grin, her gaze never wavering as Sean sauntered toward them. "And if you tell me that you don't see it, then I'm giving up on you and taking another shot at him myself."

"Okay, yes, I see it," Deanna admitted. "Now hush."

Ruby ignored her plea and leaned down to whisper, "I still say he has the hots for you. Just look at that glint in his eyes. He hasn't even glanced at me once."

"It's probably there because he knows you're talking about him," Deanna retorted with exasperation.

Fortunately, Kevin raced ahead to literally launch himself at Sean. Deanna noticed he caught her son without breaking stride, and after one last glance in her direction, he focused all of his attention on Kevin. Deanna's heart instantly melted. She liked the fact that he treated Kevin as if what he had to say was important. Ruby had been right. Sean was a man who understood a boy's desperate need for attention. She was forced to admit it was a trait that could get to her if she let it.

Because she was so shaken by the discovery that any man could have that sort of impact on her after years of general immunity to the male segment of the species, she resorted to brisk politeness when Sean finally reached them. When he held out his hand, rather than shaking it as he'd obviously expected, she slapped an envelope of cash in it.

"I really appreciate what you did for me," she said, the words stiff and formal and not nearly as grateful as she'd meant them to be. "This is half of what I owe you. I'll have the rest in another week or so."

He gazed directly into her eyes. "Yeah, well, that's something we should talk about."

Deanna blinked at his somber tone. "Meaning?" she asked, noting that he didn't put the envelope into his pocket. In fact, he looked as if he had every intention of giving it right back to her.

Sean didn't reply. Instead he glanced across the room. "Hey, Hank," he called to another fireman, who looked to be a year or two older. His craggy features weren't as handsome as Sean's, but there was a confidence about him and an irrepressible grin that would definitely appeal to most women. "How about showing my man Kevin here and his friend Ruby around the station, while Deanna and I talk? We'll catch up with you in a few minutes."

Hank's appreciative gaze swept over Ruby and his eyes lit up. Deanna noted that Ruby looked equally intrigued.

"No problem," Hank said at once, then forced his attention to Kevin. "You really like fire trucks, huh, kid?"

"You bet," Kevin said eagerly.

"Personally, I prefer the men who drive them," Ruby said, regarding Hank with frank appreciation.

Deanna took note of his broad shoulders, dark-brown eyes and only a dark shadow of hair on his shaved head. He was definitely Ruby's type—unrepentantly male.

He grinned at Ruby. "Is that so?"

Deanna shook her head as the three of them left. "Your friend is a brave man. Ruby's a wonderful friend, but she's fickle. She has a habit of discarding men like tissues when they don't live up to her ideals, and they seldom do."

Sean chuckled. "Then I think they were made for each other. Hank is a notorious flirt."

Deanna shot a look at him. "He's not married, is he?"

Sean looked hurt by the question. "Of course not. What kind of guy do you think I am? And even if he were, what's the harm in asking him to show Ruby and Kevin around the station? I didn't set them up on a date."

"Sorry," she said at once. "I overreacted. It's just that Ruby's a lot more vulnerable than she looks. Most men miss that."

Sean stared after them, his expression thoughtful. "Yeah, I imagine they do. She looks as if she could handle anything that comes along."

"When her guard's up she can," Deanna agreed.

"But she lets it down too often and too quickly?" he guessed, surprising Deanna with his insight.

"Exactly."

Sean turned back to her. "I doubt anything much

can happen between her and Hank with Kevin along as a chaperon.''

Deanna nodded. ''You're probably right. Why did you make such a point of getting rid of them, by the way?''

''Like I said, I wanted to talk to you about the money thing.'' He held out the envelope. ''I want you to take this back.''

Deanna's hackles immediately rose. ''Not a chance. And there is no 'money thing,''' she responded edgily. ''You made a loan, which was extremely generous of you, by the way. I'm paying you back. It's a business matter.''

''It's not as if we signed loan papers and there's some huge penalty if you miss a payment,'' he retorted. ''It was a hundred bucks, not a thousand. I wish it could have been more. After the fire destroyed everything you owned, I thought a few extra dollars might help you get back on your feet, buy a few essentials. I certainly didn't need it back right away.''

''Maybe in your world a hundred dollars doesn't amount to much, but it was a lifeline for me.''

''That's exactly my point. You need it right now. I don't. It's certainly not worth working yourself into exhaustion to pay me back.''

Deanna groaned. Now she understood why he'd gone all worried and protective on her. ''Ruby's been blabbing, hasn't she? Did she tell you I was working too much?''

''She mentioned two jobs and extra hours on top of that,'' he admitted. ''That's crazy.''

''It's not crazy if I want to start over and get out of her apartment.''

''Is she complaining?''

"No, of course not."

"Well then, what's the rush?"

"It's a matter of principle."

"Is the principle worth more than your son's happiness?"

Deanna stared at his suddenly harsh expression. "What kind of question is that?" she demanded heatedly. "*Nothing* is more important to me than Kevin's happiness and well-being. And what right do you have to question that? You don't even know me."

Despite her sharp response, he didn't back down. "Maybe not, but I can see what's staring me right in the face. Kevin needs his mom, not an extra few bucks for groceries."

"Maybe if you'd gone hungry you'd feel differently," she snapped.

"I have," he said bluntly. His unflinching gaze clashed with hers. "And I've gone without a mother. I'm here to tell you that there's no comparison. I would have gone hungry every night of my life, if it had meant seeing my mother again."

Deanna felt as if he'd landed a punch squarely in her gut. Even without details, that revelation explained a lot. No wonder he was taking her situation so personally.

"I'm sorry," she said at once, shaken by the raw pain in his voice. "What happened? Did she die?"

"No," he said tightly. "She and my dad walked out on me and my brothers. My brother Ryan was eight. I was six. And Mikey was four. As far as I know, they took the twins, who were only two, with them. We never saw them again."

"Oh, God, how awful," she whispered, trying to imagine a six-year-old having his entire family torn apart. What could possibly have driven his parents to do such an awful thing? Hadn't they understood the permanent emotional scars likely to be inflicted on the boys they'd left behind?

Even when she'd been at the lowest point in her life, when Kevin had been screaming all through the night with colic, and she hadn't known where their next meal was coming from, Deanna had never once considered walking away from him. He was the reason she'd had for going on. She wouldn't have allowed anything to split them up.

She started to reach out to touch the clenched muscle in Sean's arm, but after one look at his shuttered gaze, she drew back before she could make contact. "I really am sorry."

"I don't need your pity. I only told you that so you'd realize that I know what I'm talking about. Don't shortchange your kid on what really matters." He shoved the envelope back at her. "Keep the money until you really do have it to spare."

Years of stubborn pride told her to refuse to take it, but the look of despair in Sean's eyes made her relent. She put the envelope back in her purse. At the same time, it took every bit of restraint Deanna possessed not to reach out and hug the man standing beside her. He looked as lost and vulnerable as if his mother had walked out days, rather than years, ago.

"Just so you understand that Kevin's situation is not the same as yours. I'm not abandoning him," she said softly. "I would never in a million years walk out on my son."

"If he hardly ever sees you, it's the same thing," Sean insisted, clearly still drawing comparisons with his own background.

"I love my son."

"I'm sure you do. I even believe my mother loved me. That doesn't change the fact that she was gone." He regarded her with sudden urgency. "Please think about what I'm saying. I was only a year older than Kevin when my folks walked out. It's not something a kid ever gets over."

"I'll keep it in mind," she promised. "And I'm not just saying that. I really will."

Sean's intense gaze held hers. Finally he gave a nod of satisfaction. "That's good, then." But, as if he feared he'd given away too much, his expression suddenly went blank. "We should probably try to catch up with Hank. I imagine he's wondering what happened to us."

Deanna laughed at that. "I doubt he or Ruby even realize we're missing."

Sean's lips twitched, and then a slow grin spread across his face. In that instant the last of the tension between them was finally broken. "All the more reason to catch up with them," he said. "They're liable to forget that they have an impressionable kid tagging along."

"Does Kevin strike you as a boy who allows himself to be ignored for long?" she asked. "He's probably boring Hank to tears with a million and one questions about being a fireman. Ever since the day of the fire, it's all he's talked about. If he could sign up now, he would."

No sooner had the words left her mouth than the siren on one of the engines split the air with its loud wail.

"A call?" Deanna asked worriedly, glancing around for signs of men rushing to pile onto the trucks.

"Nope. I think Hank just showed Kevin how to turn on the siren," he said, leading the way to the truck in the next bay.

Instead of Kevin in the driver's seat, though, it was Ruby. Kevin was sitting next to her, giggling.

"Told you that would get them over here," he said, pointing to his mother and Sean as they approached. "Can I do it now?"

Hank turned and winked at them, then returned his gaze to Ruby. "If Ruby's willing to give you a turn, go for it, kid."

Ruby didn't budge. "I don't know. I kind of like it up here. I understand why you guys get off on this kind of thing."

"It's not driving the truck that does it," Hank explained patiently.

Ruby regarded him doubtfully. "So you don't get some macho kick out of making all that noise and tearing through the streets?"

"I never said that. But we make noise and tear through the streets to get to the fire faster," Hank said. "It's not some macho game. We're trying to save lives and property."

Ruby nodded solemnly. "Then it's the danger? You like putting your life on the line?"

"It's not as if we deliberately risk our lives for the fun of it," he retorted, his genial expression suddenly fading.

"No, for the thrill of it," Ruby corrected.

Hank regarded her with obvious exasperation. "It's about doing a job. If we do it right, there's only a tiny, carefully calculated risk involved."

Ruby grinned. "Then all those medals for bravery I heard about inside, you didn't really deserve those?"

"Oh, brother," Sean muttered. He turned to Deanna. "Want to grab Kevin and go out for a soda or something? My shift's over, and I have a hunch those two will be arguing about this for a while. Ruby's pushing all of Hank's buttons. His wife left him because she thought he was a danger junkie."

"Ouch," Deanna said. "Maybe I ought to warn her."

Sean shook his head. "Don't. His ex was right, and so is Ruby. He needs reminding occasionally." He met her gaze. "So, how about that soda?"

Deanna knew the smart thing would be to refuse, but she couldn't seem to make herself say the words. She simply nodded, then added, "But you're not going to get Kevin away from here till he gets to turn on that siren."

"Good point." Sean climbed up on the opposite side of the truck, whispered something to Kevin, then helped him to reach the button to turn on the siren. Ruby looked vaguely startled, but she never tore her gaze away from Hank. He looked equally captivated, despite his apparent frustration at the turn their conversation had taken.

"We're leaving now," Deanna announced.

"Whatever," Ruby said.

"I'll get Ruby home," Hank said absently.

"I'm perfectly capable of getting home on my own," Ruby shot back. "I walked over here, didn't I?"

Hank shot a bewildered glance toward Sean. "Was that offer an insult? I thought I was being a gentleman."

"Don't ask me," Sean said. "Everyone knows I don't understand women. You're the expert."

"Hah!" Ruby muttered.

"I heard that," Hank said.

"I meant for you to hear it."

Sean chuckled. "Okay, children, play nice. The grown-ups are leaving now."

He scooped Kevin up and settled him on his shoulders, then beckoned to Deanna. "Let's get out of here before we get caught in the crossfire."

"I don't get it," Kevin said. "Ruby really, really likes guys. How come she's been fighting with Hank the whole time we've been here? She hardly even knows him."

"Sometimes people just don't hit it off," Deanna said.

"Then how come she's staying here instead of coming with us?" Kevin asked, his expression puzzled.

"He's got you there," Sean said, amusement sparkling in his eyes.

Deanna frowned at his obvious reference to the sizzling sexual chemistry between their friends. "I don't think there's an explanation that's suitable for a five-year-old, do you?"

"How come?" Kevin asked.

"You'll understand when you're older," Sean told him, winking at Deanna.

"But I need to know now," Kevin persisted. "My teacher says you gotta ask questions if you're gonna learn stuff."

"Hard to argue with a teacher," Sean agreed. "Deanna? Care to give it a shot?"

She frowned at him. "Ruby is staying because she wants to," she told Kevin, hoping it was the kind of simple explanation that even a five-year-old could grasp and accept.

"But why?" Kevin glanced back toward Ruby. "Look. They're still arguing. What fun is that?"

"Some people think a lively argument is stimulating," Sean said. It was apparent that he was barely holding back a laugh.

Deanna regarded him with exasperation. He was clearly enjoying her discomfort with the entire topic. "Care to find out if we're among them?" she asked testily.

He did laugh at that. "Nope. I'm a nonconfrontational kind of guy."

Kevin peered quizzically at both of them. "I still don't get it," he said, sounding disgusted. His expression brightened when they reached a drugstore with an old-fashioned soda fountain inside. "Can I have a chocolate milkshake?"

Deanna would have let him have anything he wanted if it would take his mind off the byplay between Hank and Ruby that had evidently been building to some sort of sexual crescendo all evening long.

"A milkshake's fine," she said.

"What about you?" Sean asked, regarding her with continued amusement. "Something nice and tame, like a vanilla cone?"

It was obvious he was deliberately taunting her. Instantly an image of provocatively licking that ice cream just to torment him flashed through her mind. "Yes, as a matter of fact. An ice-cream cone would be lovely."

The three of them slid onto stools at the counter, with Kevin strategically set up as a buffer in the middle. Sean ordered two milkshakes and the vanilla cone.

When the order came, Deanna deliberately swiveled her stool around until she was facing Sean. He was just responding to something Kevin had asked when he caught sight of her slowly swiping her tongue over the scoop of ice cream. He literally froze, his gaze locked on her. Satisfaction and a hint of something far more dangerous swept through her.

How long had it been since she'd felt that kind of power over a man? How long since her blood had heated to a delicious sizzle under an intense gaze? Too long apparently, because panic promptly set in.

What was she doing? Was she crazy? She didn't play this kind of game. Games were Ruby's territory. Deanna didn't even understand the rules half the time.

"Mom!"

Kevin's urgent tone shook her out of her daze. "What?"

"Your ice cream's melting," he said.

Little wonder, she thought since her temperature had obviously shot into the stratosphere in the past two minutes. Instead of licking at the dripping cone as she might have done scant minutes ago, she swiped at the drips with a napkin, trying not to notice Sean's knowing expression.

"Hot night," he observed mildly.

"Yes," she agreed, her voice oddly—annoyingly—choked.

Kevin looked from one of them to the other, then shook his head. "You guys are as weird as Ruby and Hank."

Deanna was very much afraid her son had gotten it exactly right.

Chapter Four

Sean wondered what the hell had ever made him think that Deanna was innocent as a lamb? The woman was a temptress, possibly even more dangerous than the incomparable Ruby, because Deanna's seductiveness came from out of the blue.

Ever since she'd played that little game of hers with the ice-cream cone, the image had been locked in his brain. Granted, she'd looked a little rattled by the episode and had backed off almost instantly, but she'd definitely known what she was doing when she'd gazed straight into his eyes and run her tongue slowly over that melting ice cream. Even now, just thinking about it made him go hard as a rock.

He'd been working out at the gym practically nonstop on his days off, but it hadn't relieved the sexual tension one iota. There was probably only one surefire way to deal with it, but the thought of going out with some other woman—using her—to forget about Deanna was too crummy a notion to even consider. Sean tried never to behave like a complete jerk where the women in his life were concerned, no matter how willing they claimed to be to take whatever he was interested in offering.

He'd been deliberately avoiding Hank the past couple of days, as well. He didn't want to hear about any conquest that involved Ruby. Part of that was some ridiculous sense of loyalty to Deanna and her friend, part of it was self-serving. Hearing about Hank's sexual exploits would only remind him of the self-imposed drought in his own life. Moreover, he wasn't ready for the kind of probing questions Hank was likely to ask about him and Deanna. Not that there was anything to tell.

Sean finished his workout, showered and changed into comfortable jeans and a gray department-issued T-shirt. He was already thinking about the pizza he was going to order while he watched the Red Sox game when he ran smack into Hank coming in the door of the gym. His partner was unshaven and looked as if he hadn't slept a wink in days. The stubble on his shaved head was longer than he usually allowed it to get, too.

"Hey," Sean said, dragging him back outside and studying him with concern. "What's up with you? You look like hell."

"No sleep," Hank muttered, avoiding his gaze.

Sean was relatively certain he knew why. Ruby, no doubt. Dammit, just for once, why couldn't Hank have behaved in a less predictable way, maybe shown Ruby a little respect, instead of jumping her bones the first chance he got?

"Yeah, well, that's never been a problem before," he said, careful to avoid any mention of his suspicions.

"I've never been in a situation like this before," Hank said, his expression grim, rather than gloating. "Look, I need to get in there and work out for a couple of hours. Maybe if I'm exhausted enough, I'll get some sleep."

"No date tonight?"

"No," Hank said in a tone that didn't invite further questions.

"Want to come over and watch the game when you're done?" Sean asked. "I'm going to order a pizza. I'll even let you get anchovies on your half."

Hank shrugged without enthusiasm. "Sure. Why not? I'll cut it short here and be there by seven-thirty." His gaze narrowed. "No prying questions, though. Are we clear on that?"

Sean bit back his disappointment, but he nodded. Since he was no more interested in talk than Hank appeared to be, he could hardly complain about the embargo. "See you then," he said, staring after his friend as Hank trudged into the gym with all the energy and enthusiasm of a man walking toward the gallows.

Something wasn't quite right here, but Sean couldn't put his finger on it. However, given Hank's edict about keeping all his questions to himself and his own determination not to discuss Ruby with Hank, he was at a loss.

He thought about all the possible explanations for Hank's mood on the drive back to his apartment. No matter which way he looked at it, it all came back to Ruby.

Of course, there was one subtle way to get some

answers, he concluded, picking up the phone before he could change his mind. And didn't he owe it to his friend to try to pinpoint the problem? Indeed, he did, he thought nobly. He had a duty to make the call.

At the sound of Deanna's voice, his mouth went dry. What the hell was wrong with him? No woman had ever rendered him tongue-tied before.

"Um, Deanna, this is Sean."

"Hi. How are you?" she said, not even sounding particularly surprised to hear from him, much less shaken by the sound of his voice.

"Fine. Just fine. You?" he asked irritably.

"Fine."

"And Kevin?"

"He's fine."

Sean nearly groaned. Could this be any more awkward? He couldn't imagine how. "Look, I wanted to ask you about something. It's probably none of my business, but I have to admit I'm a little worried."

"About?"

"Hank," he blurted before he could think better of it.

"Oh?" she said, a wary note in her voice. "What about him?"

"Has he been seeing Ruby, I mean since the other night at the station?"

"Why don't you ask him?"

Good question, Sherlock. "Because I'm asking you," he said, unable to keep a testy note out of his tone.

"I'm not really comfortable discussing Ruby's social life with you," she said.

Sean could hardly blame her. He'd known when he picked up the phone that he was crossing some sort

of line and that he was asking her to do the same.
''It's just that I'm really worried. I've never seen him
like this.''

''Like what?''

''I can't explain it. I ran into him at the gym about
a half hour ago. He's not himself. He looks as if he's
been on a two-day bender, if you want to know the
truth, but Hank doesn't drink more than an occasional
beer, so I know it wasn't that.''

''You really are worried, aren't you?'' she asked,
sounding surprised.

''Yeah, I really am. It occurred to me that it might
have something to do with Ruby, and that if it did,
you would know about it.''

''The truth is, I don't know what's going on between them,'' Deanna admitted, her own frustration
plain. ''Ruby hasn't said much since the other night.
She's been going out as soon as I get home, then getting in late, but she hasn't said who she's with. I don't
like to pry. Usually I don't have to. She pretty much
tells me whatever's going on.''

''Sounds like Hank.''

''Sean, they're both adults,'' she said reasonably.
''I'm sure they can handle whatever's happening between them without any interference from us.''

He hesitated. ''You don't think maybe we should
get together, see if we can figure out what's going on?
They're our friends. We pretty much threw them together.''

She laughed at that. ''Please. Those two flew together like magnets. They're not our responsibility,
though I must say I'm impressed by your concern.''

Her words echoed, annoying him. *Impressed by
your concern?* Now wasn't that just about the most

boring compliment any woman had ever paid him? Sean was absurdly offended, despite the sincerity in her voice.

He sighed. What reaction had he been expecting? Had he hoped that this ridiculous excuse he'd dreamed up just to hear the sound of her voice was going to set off all sorts of bells and whistles that would have her swooning over him?

Maybe he ought to switch gears, focus on her for a change. "Okay, let's forget about Hank and Ruby for the moment. What about you? You're not working too hard, are you?"

"I imagine that depends on who you ask," she said wryly.

Sean could hear the smile in her voice. "What if I asked Ruby?"

"I thought we just agreed to leave Ruby out of this conversation."

He laughed. "Ah, then she would say you're still working too hard, wouldn't she?"

"More than likely," Deanna admitted.

"You're home early tonight."

"Joey insisted on it. I suspect Ruby got to him again. I honestly don't know how she does it, but if I ever find out, I'll put a stop to it." She sounded annoyed.

"Good for Ruby," Sean enthused. "Tell me about this restaurant. Is it any good?"

"The food's filling, and there's plenty of it. Actually the meat loaf isn't bad. And everyone seems to love the spaghetti special."

Sean pounced on the mention of his favorite food. "What night is that? I love spaghetti. My mom's was the best,'' he said, a wistful note creeping into his voice.

There were only a handful of things that could drag him right back to his childhood. Spaghetti was one of them. Ironically, when he'd first gone to his brother's pub, he'd noticed that spaghetti wasn't on the menu there. Of course, it was an Irish pub, but still, spaghetti had virtually become a universal menu item. Ryan had claimed it wasn't on the menu because he hated it. He'd also sworn that he didn't remember their mom making it. Either Ryan was lying or he'd suppressed the memory. Since Sean had done his share of that, he'd kept silent.

"You still remember your mom's spaghetti?" Deanna asked, her voice suddenly soft.

"Yeah. Silly, isn't it, when I've forgotten just about everything else about those early years. But when it comes to spaghetti, I've never had any that was better.''

"Then, by all means, come by and try Joey's sometime. It's the Thursday-night special.''

He thought about his schedule. "I'm on duty Thursday," he told her. "But maybe I can talk the guys into coming by.''

"You can leave the station?''

"As long as all of us go and take our gear with us,'' he said. "We have to be ready to roll if there's a call.''

"Well, you'll probably run into Ruby and Kevin, if you come. It's their favorite night, too.''

"I imagine if I tell that to Hank, no one will be able to keep us away.''

"Unless they've had a fight," Deanna said, sounding thoughtful. "They could have.''

"Then this will be one way to find out,'' Sean said.

"He's coming over in a few minutes. I'll mention Thursday to him."

"Okay, then. Maybe I'll see you on Thursday."

"Good night, Deanna."

"Bye."

Sean hung up the phone, then sat staring at it as if it somehow still connected them. It was an odd sensation, one he wasn't especially happy about. It had been a very long time, decades in fact, since he'd allowed himself to feel connected to anyone. Since he and his brother had hooked up, he had felt a renewed bond with Ryan, though it was still a bit on the uneasy side. And he and Hank were pretty tight, but that was it. Even the connection to his foster parents was tenuous. He still saw the Forresters from time to time, but he told himself that was because he owed them, not because he harbored any sentimental feelings toward them. The fact that there seemed to be some sort of invisible pull between him and a woman he barely knew was disconcerting.

He tried to dismiss it but knew he was only lying to himself. Why else had he called Deanna in the first place? It wasn't like him to poke around in his friend's life behind his back. It had been an excuse, pure and simple, designed to let him off the hook emotionally. He could tell himself the call had nothing to do with a ridiculously fierce longing to hear the sound of Deanna's voice.

Lies, all lies. Filled with self-disgust at the pitiful ruse, he forced himself to face facts. He was drawn to Deanna Blackwell. He shouldn't be. It was completely unwise and out of character, but there it was. He liked her. He liked her son. He was worried about the two of them.

Deanna needed a friend, he concluded. Okay, she had Ruby. But who couldn't use more than one friend? He could be that friend. And he could hang out with the kid from time to time, sort of like a big brother. It didn't have to go beyond that. He wouldn't let it go beyond that.

Satisfied with his decision, he called and ordered the pizza. But as he waited for Hank and their food to arrive, he thought of the spontaneous combustion Deanna had set off the other night simply by licking an ice cream cone, her gaze locked with his.

Friendship? *That's* all he was interested in? Yeah, right. The lies just kept piling up.

"I'll drop Kevin off at Joey's around six-thirty, and then take off," Ruby said casually as she and Deanna ate breakfast on Thursday morning.

Instantly suspicious, Deanna stared at her. "You're not having dinner? I thought you looked forward to Joey's spaghetti all week long."

Ruby shrugged. "I'm not in the mood for spaghetti."

"And at 7:00 a.m. you know that's how you're going to feel in twelve hours?"

"Yep. I'm pretty sure I'm not going to change my mind. I've been thinking about cutting back on pasta for a while now. Too many carbs."

Deanne peered at her intently. "This wouldn't have anything to do with the fact that I mentioned Hank and Sean might come by, would it?"

"Why would that matter to me?" Ruby asked, studying her cereal as if she'd never seen a bran flake before.

"That's what I'd like to know," Deanna said.

"Leave it alone," Ruby said, pushing away from the table and dumping her cereal down the garbage disposal. "I've got to get to work."

Since Ruby's job was only part-time assistant in the same neighborhood law firm where Deanna worked days as a receptionist, something was off here. Deanna could have let it alone, but it wasn't in her nature. She might not pry into Ruby's social life, but she did pay attention when her friend was behaving weirdly.

"We never leave the house before seven-thirty," she pointed out. "We're not due at the office till eight. It takes us five minutes to walk to work. What's the sudden rush? Are you trying to avoid talking to me?"

Ruby evaded Deanna's direct gaze. "I'm filling in for Cassandra this week, remember?"

"So?"

"I've got a lot of typing piled up. I'm not as fast as she is, and I still need to get out so I can be home when Kevin gets here after school."

Deanna's gaze narrowed at the mention of her son. "Is baby-sitting Kevin getting to be a problem?"

"Of course not!" Ruby said, staring at her indignantly. "Don't you dare think that. You know I love that kid as if he were my own. Heck, I've been around since the day he was born."

"Well, something's going on here," Deanna said, studying Ruby thoughtfully. She decided to go for broke and throw her suspicions on the table. "You haven't been yourself for days now, not since the night you got together with Hank at the fire station."

"One thing has nothing to do with the other," Ruby insisted, her jaw set stubbornly.

Deanna wasn't buying it, but she couldn't very well drag the truth out of Ruby if she wasn't willing to share it. "Okay," she said at last. "I'll drop it for now, on one condition."

"Anything that will get you to back off," Ruby agreed.

"Have dinner at Joey's tonight."

"Dee!" Ruby protested.

Deanna held firm. "That's it. That's my condition. Otherwise, you'll never be able to convince me that Hank's not at the bottom of your weird mood."

Something that might have been a tiny flicker of relief passed across Ruby's face, then gave way to an air of resignation. "Okay, okay. Geez, you are such a nag."

Deanna grinned at her. "I should be. I learned from the best."

Ruby shook her head. "Obviously I should have kept that lesson to myself."

Sean and five other firefighters in uniform piled into Joey's Italian Diner around six o'clock. Deanna was just coming out of the kitchen with an order when they arrived. She heard her son's whoop of delight, but missed the fact that he was racing straight across the restaurant toward Sean. He bumped into her at full throttle, knocking her off-balance and sending the tray of spaghetti dinners tilting toward disaster.

"Whoa!" Sean said, rescuing the tray in midair and managing to keep Deanna upright at the same time. He stared down into her eyes. "Are you okay?"

Deanna gazed up into blue eyes bright with amusement and felt her knees go weak again. "Having you come to my rescue is getting to be a habit," she told Sean, then turned to her son and scolded, "Kevin, you know you're supposed to watch where you're going in here.''

"Sorry, Mom!" Kevin said. "I didn't see you. I was excited to see Sean."

Deanna could relate to the feeling. A part of her hadn't expected him to actually show up, not because he was likely to change his mind but because of the unpredictability of his job. "There should be a table for six opening up in a minute," she told him as she reached for the tray. "Let me serve these dinners, and as soon as it's clear, I'll get it ready for you."

Sean held tight to the tray. "Where do you want this? It weighs a ton."

"I'm used to it," she protested.

His stubborn gaze clashed with hers. "Where?"

She shrugged and gestured toward a stand across the room. "Over there, by that table in the corner. Kevin, go on back to your table, before someone else gets tripped up."

Kevin regarded her with disappointment. "But, Mom..."

"I'll see you before I go," Sean promised him. "If your mom says it's okay, you can come have dessert with me and the guys."

Kevin's eyes lit up. "Really? And you'll tell me all about fighting fires? I want to be a fireman when I grow up, so I need to start learning stuff."

This wasn't the first Deanna had heard about her son's career plans, but she wondered how Sean was going to respond to Kevin's blatant hero worship. Glancing at him, she realized she needn't have worried. He grinned and assured Kevin he could ask all the questions he wanted. The last traces of Kevin's scowl promptly faded. Deanna had to admit, Sean had a definite way with her son. Still balancing the heavy tray on one hand, he ruffled Kevin's hair with his other hand.

"Do what your mom said," he urged Kevin. "I need to take this tray where she wants it, before she docks my pay."

Kevin giggled. "You don't work here."

"Not usually," Sean agreed. "But it's always good for a man to help out a lady, even when she doesn't think she needs any help."

Deanna caught the subtle message about her independent streak. She didn't say another word as Sean carried the tray across the room. She noted that several fascinated gazes followed his progress. Well aware of how the elderly regulars liked to take an interest in her social life, she knew she'd be hearing about the incident for days to come.

"I can take it from here," she told him when he'd set the tray down.

Sean glanced at the tray, which held only specials. He winked at the elderly woman closest to him. "I imagine this is yours," he said, then leaned down to whisper. "She doesn't think I know what I'm doing, so help me out here okay?"

Mrs. Wiley beamed at him. "Crazy girl," she said with a *tsk* for Deanna's benefit. "I can't imagine what she's thinking, turning down the help of a big, strong firefighter. You put that plate right here, young man."

Deanna stood back while he served all four women, who were giggling at his teasing as if they were thirty years younger. When all the dinners were on the table, he stood back and surveyed the results with evident pride.

"Not such a bad job, if I do say so myself," he said. "I didn't spill a drop."

"Only one problem," Deanna noted mildly, barely containing a grin. "These dinners were destined for that table over there."

She gestured toward two couples who were watching the scene from the next table. Three of the four looked amused, but the fourth looked as if he were about to burst a blood vessel.

Mrs. Wiley patted Sean's hand. "Oh, don't mind them, young man. You did a fine job. We'll send over a bottle of Joey's house wine and they won't complain."

Sean looked chagrined. "I'll buy the wine," he said, turning to the other group. "Sorry. I was trying to be helpful."

Amazingly, Mr. Horner, who usually complained about everything, simply shrugged, his anger defused. "Long as you don't expect a big tip, I imagine we can wait."

Sean winced and turned to Deanna. "Sorry."

She was tempted to make him squirm, but he looked so miserable, she relented. "He's a lousy tipper, anyway," she whispered. "By the way, I see that Joey has cleared that table for you. It might be a good idea if you went over there now before I lose all my tips for the night."

Sean retreated to the table where the other firefighters had been seated. Deanna had deliberately sent them to a table that was not part of her station, so she could escape Sean's watchful gaze. Let Adele cope with them. There hadn't been a customer born who could fluster her.

The tactic was only partially successful. Deanna still

felt Sean's gaze following her as she worked her way
between tables, joking with the customers, carrying
orders from the frantic kitchen and helping to clear
tables for the line of customers waiting to be seated.

It was so busy for a couple of hours that she was
only dimly aware that the firefighters didn't seem to
be in any big rush to leave. Hank had slipped away
from his table and joined Ruby, trading places with
Kevin, who was basking in the undivided attention of
Sean and the other firefighters, all of whom were being
incredibly patient with his endless barrage of questions.

By eight, the crowd finally started to thin out. Those
remaining were lingering over coffee and Joey's chocolate cannoli. Satisfied that things in the dining room
were under control for the moment, Deanna slipped
onto a stool in the kitchen and kicked off her shoes
with a sigh of pleasure.

"It's about time you had a break," Sean said, appearing beside her with a frown on his face. "Have
you eaten?"

"I grabbed something earlier," she told him.

"Earlier when?" he asked, his skepticism plain.
"Lunchtime?"

"Actually I had some salad not more than twenty
minutes ago."

"Meaning she grabbed a carrot on her way through
the kitchen," the cook chimed in helpfully.

Deanna scowled at Victor, who was ogling Sean
with frank appreciation. "Traitor," she accused him.

Victor grinned. "Given a choice between you and
your gorgeous friend, whose side did you think I'd be
on?"

Deanna chuckled as Sean regarded Victor uneasily.

"Don't panic," she advised Sean. "He's almost as harmless as Ruby. He's also been in a long-term relationship with the same man for years now."

"Good to know," Sean said. "Now let's get back to you. You need to eat. Victor, can you fix something for her?"

Deanna bristled at his commanding tone. "*If* I wanted something to eat, which I don't, I could fix it myself. Victor doesn't have to wait on me."

Sean frowned at her. "Don't be stubborn. You have to be starving."

"Sean, I've been taking care of myself and my son for a long time now. Neither one of us is malnourished. Doesn't that tell you something?"

Victor looked from Sean's set jaw to Deanna's equally set expression and immediately headed for the door. "Think I'll go ask Joey to fix me a cappuccino. You two decide you want anything, help yourselves."

"We won't," Deanna said tightly.

As soon as they were alone, she whirled on Sean. "What do you think you're doing coming into a place I work and bossing me around?"

He looked bemused by her reaction. "All I did was suggest you should have something to eat."

"*Suggest?* That's not how I heard it. You practically ordered me to eat. I don't get it. Why are my eating habits any of your business?"

He jammed his hands in his pockets and backed off a step. "Okay, you're right. They're not."

"Then what's going on?"

"Someone needs to look out for you."

"Someone *does*," she retorted. "Me. That's how it's been for a long time now."

"Well, pardon me for caring," he snapped defensively.

Deanna was taken aback by his choice of words and by the expression on his face. He looked as if he hated how he was acting almost as much as she did.

She bit back her irritation and managed to keep her voice level as she asked, "Sean, what's really going on here?"

"I wish to hell I knew," he muttered. "You obviously don't want me interfering in your life. I really don't want to be in your life, yet here I am."

"I didn't ask you to come here tonight," she reminded him. "It was your idea."

He scowled. "Don't you think I know that?"

"Then I'm afraid I don't get it." She looked into his eyes and saw evidence of the internal struggle he was waging with himself. She softened her voice. "Sean?"

He kept his gaze locked with hers for what seemed to be an eternity. She could hear the tick of the clock on the kitchen wall, the sighing of the refrigerators switching on, the clink of ice in the automated ice maker.

"Oh, what the hell?" he murmured, reaching for her and slanting his mouth over hers.

He caught her by surprise. The kiss was the absolute last thing she expected when he was so clearly exasperated with her and annoyed with himself. He claimed her lips with a heady combination of heat and urgency that had her breath snagging in her throat and her senses spinning wildly.

Then, almost as quickly as it had started, it was over. Sean raked a hand impatiently through his hair and regarded her with regret.

"I'm sorry," he said, turning on his heels and leaving before Deanna could gather her wits to reply.

She stared after him, wondering what the apology was for...their argument or the kiss.

Please don't let it be for the kiss, she thought wildly, touching a shaky finger to her lips. It had been a very long time since any man had kissed her like that, and she'd been perfectly content to let it stay that way.

Until now. With one kiss Sean Devaney had unwittingly awakened a sleeping need in her. She might not want him telling her what to do or fretting over her eating habits, but, heaven help her, she definitely wanted him to kiss her again. Soon.

Chapter Five

Kissing Deanna had to qualify as one of the ten dumbest things he'd ever done in his life, Sean concluded on the ride back to the station. He hadn't meant to kiss her. He hadn't wanted to kiss her.

The shouts of *liar* that echoed in his head at that claim were way too loud to be ignored. Okay then, he had *wanted* to kiss her from the very first instant when he'd had to steady her and that tray after her near run-in with her son. Two seconds of contact with all those soft, yielding curves and he'd wanted even more than a kiss. He'd wanted to drag her into his arms and discover every single secret of her delectable body. It had been a long time since he'd felt that kind of instantaneous rush of pure lust.

But he'd dealt with that impulsive, totally male response during dinner. He'd lectured himself on the sheer folly of any intimate contact with her. He'd joined in the speculative jokes his buddies were making about Hank and Ruby. He'd focused intently on Kevin's apparently endless barrage of questions. He'd teased their waitress, pleaded for Joey's surprisingly incredible recipe for spaghetti sauce. He'd done everything he could think of to get his mind completely off Deanna.

He'd done all that, but he hadn't been able to keep his eyes off her. She was always at the periphery of his vision. The sound of her laughter was always teasing him, drawing his focus away from his friends. Hell, he could almost swear he could even pick out the scent of her perfume when she was two aisles away. How pathetic was that?

Given all that, it was little wonder he was destined to cave in to insanity when he followed her into the kitchen. One instant he'd been defending himself against her fury over his overbearing attitude, the next he'd been hauling her into his arms to silence her with a mind-numbing kiss. He was surprised she hadn't slugged him.

Of course, that could be because she'd been too stunned, he thought, a grin tugging at his lips. He recalled her dazed expression when he'd brusquely apologized and walked away. A tiny, satisfied sensation stole through him. God, he was such a *man,* he thought with disgust, taking pleasure in having caught a woman off guard and having gotten her to respond to him. Responses earned that way didn't mean anything. Not really, anyway.

"What's your problem?" Hank asked, joining him in the sleeping quarters where Sean had retreated when they got back to the fire station.

"Nothing," Sean lied, deliberately stretching out on

top of the sheets as if he'd just come in to catch a quick nap.

"Woman troubles," Hank assessed knowingly. His own mood seemed to be much improved. "You and Deanna have a fight?"

Sean ignored the question. "You and Ruby make up?"

"Ruby and I never fought."

"Could have fooled me," Sean said.

Hank's gaze narrowed. "And you're deliberately changing the subject. Why is that, I wonder? You've been uptight as hell ever since you came out of the kitchen at the restaurant. Did Deanna tell you to get lost?"

That could be one interpretation of her angry diatribe about his meddling in her life, Sean decided. But if her words had held him at a distance, the way she'd returned his kiss had been the exact opposite.

Geez, what was happening to him? He was hanging around his bunk pondering the implications of a stupid kiss. He never did stuff like this. A woman kissed him or she didn't. She slept with him or she didn't. Her choice, always. He never got hung up over it one way or the other. That Deanna had him weighing the meaning of it all was a very bad sign. It was time to run for the hills.

But he didn't want to run anywhere...except straight back to the restaurant so he could kiss her again and make sure that the wicked wonder of the first time had been real.

Deanna sat at Ruby's kitchen table with her jar of tips and began sorting the money. She did it once a month, then deposited the cash into her savings account, the one she'd started when she'd been convinced that if she planned ahead she could put enough money aside to buy a little house someday for herself and Kevin. The costs associated with getting back on her feet after the fire had wiped out every last penny she'd accumulated to that point.

Kevin wandered into the kitchen, his eyes widening at the sight of all the wrinkled dollar bills and change. "Wow," he said, climbing into a chair opposite her and propping his elbows on the table for a closer look. "That's a lot of money. Are we rich finally?"

She smiled at the question. "Hardly."

He studied her thoughtfully. "Do we have enough to get our own place yet?"

Deanna's head snapped up at the plaintive note behind the question. "What's wrong? I thought you liked staying here with Ruby."

"Sure," he said at once. "Ruby's the best."

"Then what's the problem?"

"I was thinking maybe if you and me had our own place, Sean would come to see us."

It wasn't the first time Sean's name had come up around the house. Kevin had been quoting him nonstop since the fire. Going to the fire station and then seeing him at Joey's had only reinforced his hero worship. In Kevin's view, Sean Devaney pretty much hung the moon. Deanna knew allowing that to continue carried risks, but she didn't want to steal the one bright spot in her son's life. Still, she had to caution him against expecting too much.

"Honey, you can't expect Sean to come around. He has his own life."

"But he likes me. He said so."

"He's also a very busy man. He has an important

job, and I'm sure he has his own grown-up friends that he likes to spend time with when he's off. I don't think he's staying away because we live with Ruby.''

"But I'm his friend, too," Kevin said reasonably. "And if we had our own place, I could invite him to dinner. He'd come. I know he would, especially if you fixed spaghetti like Joey's.''

"Then he did like it?" Deanna asked. She'd wondered about that. She'd intended to ask him, but they'd gotten sidetracked in the kitchen. She nearly groaned at the understatement. They'd gotten more than sidetracked. Every rational thought in her head had flown straight out the window when he'd kissed her. Even now, just thinking about the way his mouth had felt on hers, she had to drag her attention back to Kevin.

"Uh-huh," he said. "Sean said it was the best spaghetti he'd had since he was a little kid. So if you promised to fix it, I know he'd come for dinner.''

Deanna sighed. "Kevin, you know that I'm not even home for dinner most nights. That wouldn't be any different if we had our own place.''

His expression turned mulish. "You never want me to have my friends over.''

A headache was beginning to pound at his relentless complaining. "Sweetie, that's not true," she said, trying to keep her voice even.

"It is so true," he insisted. "You always say I can have them over when you're here, but you're never here.''

Deanna considered the accusation and realized it was possible Kevin had gotten it exactly right. She always meant to let him invite his friends over, but there were simply too few free hours in her week, and she didn't want Ruby to have to baby-sit Kevin's friends. It was enough that she was willing to look after Kevin.

"Why don't you go call them right now and ask them to come over?" she suggested. "We can order a pizza."

"I don't want a pizza. I want Sean to come over," Kevin said, clearly impatient that she'd missed his point.

"Not today," she said flatly.

"Then can I go see him at the fire station again?"

"No."

"Why not?" he asked, clearly warming to this new idea. "I could call first and ask if it's okay. If you can't go, Ruby would probably take me. She probably wants to see Hank, anyway." His expression turned serious. "I still don't get why they fight so much, but I think she really, really likes Hank, don't you? And he's kinda cool, not as cool as Sean, but okay."

Deanna wished she could be as sure of Ruby's feelings as Kevin seemed to be, but Ruby never mentioned the man's name. That might be a dead giveaway that she cared...or it might mean the opposite, that she hadn't given him a thought. It wasn't as if he was hanging around, at least not while Deanna was around. And since Ruby didn't have a phone at the apartment, the two of them couldn't be spending hours on the phone talking, either.

When she didn't respond to Kevin's question, he slid his chair closer. "So, is it okay? Can I call Sean?"

Deanna knew she ought to nip this whole thing in the bud, but the hopeful expression in Kevin's eyes kept her from saying no outright. After all, Sean was a grown man. If Kevin was making a nuisance of himself, Sean could find some way to tell him not to come

by the station. And Ruby knew how to protect herself
if she wanted to steer clear of Hank. She certainly
hadn't seemed all that upset that he'd joined her after
dinner the other night at Joey's. Every time Deanna
had glanced their way, the two of them had been
laughing.

She reached over and brushed Kevin's hair off his
forehead. He needed a haircut, but he'd refused, telling
her he wanted his hair to be as long as Sean's.
"Okay," she relented. "If Ruby doesn't mind taking
you, ask her to go to the pay phone with you and you
can call." She tossed him enough change for the
phone.

"All right!" Kevin said, bounding out of the
kitchen. "I'm gonna call right now."

"Ask Ruby first!" Deanna shouted after him. "And
take her with you. Do not go to the corner by yourself."

"Ask Ruby what?" Ruby inquired, appearing in the
kitchen doorway.

"If you're willing to take him to the fire station for
a visit if Sean says it's okay." Deanna studied her
reaction. Ruby's expression remained completely neutral. "You're not answering me."

"Sure, I'll take him," Ruby said with a shrug. "It's
no big deal. Why can't you take him, though?"

"Because that's a bad idea," Deanna said without
thinking.

Ruby regarded her with sudden fascination. "Oh,
really?"

"I meant that I have things to do."

"That is not what you meant," Ruby accused.
"You meant that you don't want to see Sean Devaney

again. Why is that? He seems like a perfectly nice guy to me."

"He is a nice guy," Deanna conceded reluctantly.

"Then what's the problem?" Ruby studied her face. "Or do I even need to ask? Are you beginning to see that he's more than just a nice guy? Are you maybe just the teensiest bit attracted to him?"

"If I admit that I am, will you leave me alone?"

Ruby's grin spread. "For the moment," she agreed. "I will, however, point out that that makes you a complete and total coward for refusing to take Kevin to the fire station."

Deanna looked straight into Ruby's eyes. "Maybe I'm just playing hard to get."

"As if," Ruby scoffed. "You don't play at that. With you it's the real thing." She regarded Deanna with evident fascination. "Have you kissed him yet?"

Deanna was debating the technical accuracy of a negative response, when Ruby gasped as if she'd just read her mind. "My God, I've got that backward, haven't I? He's kissed you."

"Once," Deanna admitted reluctantly.

Ruby studied her with undisguised curiosity. "Well, tell all. How was it? Was it awful? Is that why you don't want to see him?"

"No, it was not awful," Deanna said. "How could it be? We're talking about Sean Devaney here."

Ruby held a hand to her chest. "Oh, my, that good, huh? When did it happen? Never mind. I think I know. It was when he followed you into the kitchen at Joey's. That's why you looked completely dazed when you finally wandered out of there, isn't it?"

"I did not look dazed," Deanna said with exasperation.

"I just call 'em like I see 'em," Ruby retorted. "Well, well, well…this is definitely a fascinating turn of events. Is Sean the first man who's gotten close enough to kiss you since Frankie?"

"Don't be absurd. Frankie's been gone for more than five years. Of course other men have kissed me." Joey. Old Mr. Jenkins at the restaurant. Even one of the law partners at work had given her a friendly peck on the cheek once when they'd said goodbye after an office party.

"Why is my head screaming 'Technicality' when you say that?" Ruby demanded. "I'll rephrase. Has any sexy man kissed you with mind-blowing passion since Frankie?"

Deanna sighed. "You've been hanging out with lawyers for too long."

"Dee?"

"You're relentless."

"Yes, as a matter of fact, I am," Ruby said with pride. "Well?"

"Okay, no."

"You did kiss him back, didn't you? You didn't freeze up or, worse yet, slug him?"

"Oh, no," Deanna said, feeling her cheeks flood with heat. "I definitely kissed him back."

Ruby beamed. "This just gets better and better."

"It was a kiss," Deanna reminded her. "It lasted all of thirty seconds, tops. Then he apologized and bolted out of the kitchen."

"Smart man," Ruby said with approval.

"Smart?"

"Always leave 'em wanting more. I think that's especially applicable in your case. If he'd swooped in for another kiss, you probably would have slugged him.''

Deanna regarded her with dismay. ''I do not make a habit of slugging men.''

''Only because none prior to this have been brave enough to ignore the Do Not Touch warnings posted all around you.''

Deanna took an exaggerated look around. ''I don't see any signs.''

''Trust me. Men do. Our Sean is a very brave man. He gets my vote.''

''Vote for what?''

''Guy you're most likely to sleep with.''

Deanna ignored the fluttering that Ruby's words set off in the pit of her stomach and held up her hand. ''Hold it right there. It's a pretty big leap from letting the man kiss me once to hopping into bed with him.''

''Sometimes yes, sometimes no,'' Ruby replied knowingly. ''I'm betting it's not much more than a baby step for Sean.''

''Then isn't it a good thing I don't intend to see him again?'' Deanna shot back.

''Coward,'' Ruby accused softly.

Deanna met her friend's direct gaze without flinching. ''Darn straight.''

For nearly a month now, Deanna had been going out of her way to avoid him, Sean concluded when Kevin and Ruby showed up at the fire station without her yet again. It was getting on his nerves. So was watching this bizarre dance Hank and Ruby seemed to be doing. They barely spoke. Hank merely watched her as if she possessed the key to eternal youth.

After observing this same ritual for an entire afternoon, Sean finally decided he'd had enough. Since Hank wouldn't answer his questions, he decided to try Ruby. He sent Kevin off to the kitchen to bring back sodas for all of them.

"You and Hank have a fight?" he inquired as casually as possible.

Ruby regarded him with an unflinching gaze. "No. Why do you ask?"

Sean shrugged, uncomfortable in his unfamiliar role as meddler. "Seemed for a while as if you two were really hitting it off. Now it doesn't."

Her expression brightened. "Sort of like you and Deanna?"

He frowned at that. "Who said anything about Deanna?"

"Since we're discussing our personal lives, I figured it was a fair question. You going to ask her out?"

Sean was flustered by the question. "I hadn't thought about it."

"Why not? Didn't you enjoy kissing her?" Ruby asked bluntly.

He groaned. He'd thought that was a relatively well-kept secret. "She told you about that?"

"Not willingly," Ruby admitted with a grin. "I pried it out of her."

He shoved his hands in his pockets and wished he had the power to make himself sink through the floor. "Yeah, well, that was probably a mistake."

"Me prying or you kissing?"

He chuckled despite himself. "Probably both."

"You regret kissing her?" she asked, clearly disappointed. "Because I don't think she does. I think she's scared, not sorry."

Sean was intrigued by her interpretation. "Why would she be scared?"

"Because she hasn't dated much since Frankie left. The scumbag really destroyed her self-confidence, if you know what I mean. She doesn't trust her own judgment when it comes to men, so she avoids all of them."

Sean studied her with a narrowed gaze. "Is there a point to all this insight you're sharing with me?"

"Just that you're the first guy she's shown any interest in. Add to that the fact you're a nice guy, and that makes you the perfect candidate to help her get her feet wet." She surveyed him closely. "Unless that kiss scared you, too. Is that it, Sean? Are you as much of a coward as she is?"

Sean ignored the taunt. "Who told you I was a nice guy?"

"Nobody told me. I *am* a good judge of men. Not that you could tell it by the one I married, but I learned a lot from that mistake. My standards have improved."

"Is that why you ended things with Hank?"

She regarded him with surprise. "Who said I ended things with Hank?"

"I just thought..."

"You thought I'd dumped him because I figured out that he's a big flirt."

"To be honest, yes."

Ruby patted his cheek. "Honey, that just makes him a challenge," she said.

Shaking his head, Sean watched her as she sashayed off toward the kitchen in search of Kevin. He had to give her credit. She understood Hank probably better than Hank understood himself, which raised an interesting point. Did she understand *him,* too? *Was* he avoiding Deanna because he was a coward?

Yep, no question about it. With his reputation on the line, he picked up the phone on the wall, took a slip of wrinkled paper from his pocket and dialed her number at the restaurant. He was relieved when Deanna was the one who answered on the first ring.

"Ruby, is that you?"

"No, it's Sean."

"Oh."

"I thought maybe we could go out for dinner sometime. Are you interested?"

Silence greeted the blunt question, then she finally demanded, "Did Ruby put you up to this?"

Sean chuckled. "Sweetheart, Ruby may be able to manipulate your pal Joey, but she doesn't get to me."

"That doesn't mean she didn't try. I know she and Kevin are over there."

"Look, leave Ruby out of this. It's a simple question. Would you like to have dinner with me sometime or not? Yes or no?"

"You could come by Joey's," she conceded eventually. "We could eat together when I take my break."

Sean bit back a grin at her attempt to avoid being on a real date with him. "As attractive as that offer is, I think I'd prefer a time and place when I can have your undivided attention."

"Why?"

Sean barely smothered a laugh. He was tempted to suggest that she must not date much if she couldn't figure out the answer to that one herself, but he decided that would probably just infuriate her. If Ruby was telling him the truth, she really *didn't* date much.

"So we'll have time to talk," he said instead.

"About what?" she asked suspiciously.

This time he did laugh. "The weather. Kevin. Hank and Ruby. The Red Sox. Whatever we decide we want to talk about. We're adults. We have varied backgrounds. The possibilities are endless."

"Oh."

"Deanna, this isn't a trap," he said gently. "I just thought you might enjoy a night out with somebody waiting on *you* for a change. There's no hidden agenda." He hesitated, then, unable to resist teasing her just a bit, he added, "I won't even kiss you again unless you ask me to."

He waited for a response, but she remained perfectly quiet. "Would you be more interested if I said I *would* kiss you?" he asked.

She laughed, although it sounded to him as if her laughter was a little choked.

"That's what I was waiting to hear, of course," she said gamely. She drew in a deep breath. "This invitation of yours—it's not very specific. Are you just testing the waters, or did you have a particular night in mind?"

"First night we're both free," he said at once, ridiculously pleased that she was considering the invitation. "I'm off tonight and tomorrow night, then again over the weekend. How's your schedule?"

"I'm working tonight and tomorrow night and over the weekend," she said.

"Including Sunday night?"

"No. Actually I'm off by three on Sunday afternoon, but I'm usually pretty beat. I don't know what kind of company I'd be. And that's usually the time I reserve for Kevin."

"Then bring him along," Sean said, seizing on the

excuse to avoid risking another one of those sizzling kisses. "I don't mind."

"You don't?"

"Of course not," he said with total sincerity. "He's a terrific kid. Besides, you know I'd be the last person to want to steal some of your time with him."

"Then Sunday sounds good," she said.

"I'll pick you up at five. We'll make it an early evening, since Kevin has school the next day." It also meant less time with Deanna on a sultry spring night when the senses tended to take over.

"Perfect," she said, sounding oddly relieved, as well.

If they weren't a sorry pair, Sean thought wryly as he hung up. He wasn't sure which of them was worse. Bottom line, they were both cowards.

Which raised an interesting point. Neither of them would have a thing to fear if there were no attraction at work between them. That meant they were both terrified for a reason. And it went back to that kiss.

So, he concluded happily, he had absolutely nothing to fear as long as he didn't kiss her again.

Of course, as soon as he hit on that as the perfect solution, the desire to do the exact opposite and kiss her senseless slammed into him and wouldn't let go. Sunday night began to loom as a monumental test of his willpower. He had this gut-deep feeling he was going to lose.

Chapter Six

Ruby listened to Deanna's announcement that Sean was taking her and Kevin out to dinner on Sunday without saying a word.

"Well, say something," Deanna finally said. "I thought you'd be dancing around the room. This is what you've been hoping for, isn't it?"

"Actually, what I was hoping for was you and Sean, all alone in some romantic setting where you could pick up where that kiss left off," Ruby retorted. "Have you lost your mind? The first sexy man you've been attracted to in years asks you on a date, and you're taking your five-year-old son along?"

Deanna frowned. "Sean didn't seem to mind."

"No, I don't imagine he did," Ruby scoffed. "He may be the only person in Boston more terrified than you are of having a real relationship."

"And you reached this conclusion how?"

"By talking to him," Ruby explained with exaggerated patience. "It's a fascinating concept. You should try it sometime."

They were interrupted by the sound of the buzzer from downstairs.

"That's probably Sean," Deanna said, actually relieved by the interruption. For once, seeing Sean seemed preferable to listening to any more of Ruby's analysis of her cowardice. "Will you get it, while I go and hurry Kevin along?"

"If it weren't for the fact that your son would be disappointed by having to stay home after you've promised him an evening with his hero, I would never let you get away with this," Ruby said, her expression grim.

Deanna frowned at her. "It's not your call."

Ruby sighed. "No, sadly, that's true." She waved Deanna out of the room. "Go. Fetch Kevin. I'll get the door. Maybe I'll have more luck explaining to Sean how real, grown-up dates are supposed to work."

"Don't even think about it," Deanna warned, almost afraid to leave her friend alone with Sean. Ruby rarely hesitated to speak her mind.

"Oh, go on," Ruby ordered. "I promise I won't embarrass you."

Deanna left the room reluctantly. To her relief, when she returned—without Kevin, who was still in the bathroom—Ruby and Sean were discussing baseball, not the rules of dating.

"Hank's a big baseball fan, too," Sean said, his expression completely innocent. "Maybe we could all go to a Red Sox game sometime."

"Sure," Ruby said easily, surprising Deanna with her ready agreement.

Sean seemed taken aback, as well, but he rallied quickly. "I'll talk to Hank and work on getting the tickets, then. You and Kevin up for it, Deanna?"

"Kevin would be thrilled," Deanna said honestly.

Sean's gaze locked with hers. "And you?"

She flushed under the intensity of his gaze. "Sure. I'd love to go." What could be safer than a ballpark, surrounded by thousands of screaming fans, one of them her five-year-old son? If there was a way for Kevin to continue seeing Sean from time to time that wouldn't put her heart at risk, she was willing to consider it.

She caught the knowing glint in Sean's eyes and realized he had a pretty good idea of exactly what was going through her mind. Before she could think of some way to extricate herself, Kevin thundered down the hall and launched himself at Sean.

"This is so cool," he said from his perch on Sean's shoulder. "Where are we gonna go?"

"That's up to you and your mom," Sean told him. "What kind of food do you like?"

"I like pizza," Kevin said at once.

"I think we can do better than pizza tonight," Sean said, his gaze steady on Deanna. "How about seafood? Or Chinese?"

"Mom likes Chinese," Kevin admitted, his face scrunched up in disgust. "I think it's yucky."

Sean laughed. "Okay then, no Chinese food. Steak? Burgers?"

"A great burger sounds good to me," Deanna said. That would mean the kind of casual place where Kevin would feel comfortable and she wouldn't have to worry quite so much about him misbehaving. They hadn't been to a lot of fancy restaurants, not on her income. Joey's was the cream of the crop, and most of the regulars there considered Kevin a surrogate grandson.

"Then I know just the spot," Sean told her. "It's not too far from here. We can walk."

For the life of her Deanna couldn't think of a single good hamburger place in the neighborhood, but she trailed along beside Sean, content to listen to her son's nonstop barrage of questions and Sean's patient responses. She tried to imagine Frankie showing such patience and couldn't. It was a solid reminder that those occasional regrets she had about his absence from his son's life were wasted.

"Here we are," Sean announced as they reached an apartment building half a dozen blocks from her place.

Deanna gave him a quizzical look.

"There's no place in town that makes a hamburger any better than mine," he said. "And it just so happens that I went grocery shopping earlier." He studied her intently. "You okay with this?"

She managed to nod. The truth was that she felt a small quiver of anticipation in the pit of her stomach at the prospect of seeing where he lived. The building was certainly unpretentious, but the lawn around it was well tended. There were flowers blooming in pots beside the front door. A half dozen children were playing catch on the stretch of grass. She saw Kevin studying them enviously.

Apparently, Sean saw the same thing. He waved at the kids. "Hey, Davey, Mark, come on over here."

Two dark-haired boys broke away from the others and ran to Sean, regarding him with the same adulation that was usually evident on Kevin's face, though these boys were around ten or twelve.

"This is my friend Kevin," Sean told them. "Would you mind letting him play with you guys while I'm getting our dinner ready? Is that okay with you, Deanna? He'll be fine. Davey and Mark are very responsible. They look out for their kid brothers all the time."

"It's okay with us," one of the boys replied.

"Please, Mom?" Kevin begged.

She grinned at his eagerness to abandon the adults—even his beloved Sean—in favor of playing catch with some older boys. "If Sean thinks it's okay and the boys don't mind, it's fine with me."

"All right!" Kevin said, racing after the others as they loped back to their game.

Deanna stood looking after him. He was growing up so fast, and she was missing so much of it, thanks to her work schedule. In that instant she could see as plainly as she ever had that she was shortchanging not only Kevin but herself. Unfortunately, she couldn't see any way around it, not unless the courts managed to track down the errant Frankie and extract all the child-support payments he'd missed over the years.

"You don't need to worry about Kevin. Davey and Mark live right downstairs from me. Their mom keeps an eye on them out her window, and you'll be able to see them from my kitchen window, too."

Deanna forced a smile. "I'm being silly and over-protective, aren't I?"

"No, of course not. You can never be too careful in this day and age, but this neighborhood is as safe as any in town. I wouldn't have suggested letting Kevin play if it weren't. And there's always a parent within earshot."

Deanna studied him closely, realizing with a sense

of amazement that he took the safety of all these children as personally as if they were his own. "Something tells me you keep a close eye on things when
you're around, as well."

He shrugged. "I do what I can. Now let's get out
of here before we cramp their style." Reaching for her
hand, he led her inside and up the narrow stairs.

"The kitchen's this way," he said as soon as they'd
walked into his apartment.

Deanna wondered at his eagerness to keep her from
looking around. "Did you forget to straighten up this
morning?" she asked, deliberately lagging behind
him.

Sean stopped and stared at her, evidently bewildered
by the teasing question. "What?"

"You seem to be in a rush to get me into the
kitchen. I figure that's because you left your under-
wear scattered all over or something."

"Hey, I'm no slob," he protested with feigned indignation. "I thought you'd be in a hurry to look outside and check on Kevin, make sure you could keep
an eye on him."

"You told me he'd be safe," she reminded him.

"And you trust my judgment?"

"When it comes to my son, yes," she said, surprised to realize that it was true. If there was one thing
she believed with all her heart, it was that Sean would
never deliberately put her child—any child—at risk.
She was surprised by the expression that washed over
his face. Relief, maybe. Even a hint of wonder.

"Just like that?" he asked.

"Not just like that," she countered, astounded that
he would doubt her faith in his reliability. "I've seen
you with Kevin several times now. I saw how those

boys outside look up to you. And I've talked to you myself. You're a good guy, Sean, especially when it comes to kids.''

''Thanks. It means a lot to hear you say that.''

''Why? You have to know you're great with kids.''

''I don't know about that,'' he said.

''Of course you are,'' she insisted. ''You know what surprises me, though?''

''What?''

''As much as you obviously love children, I can't believe you don't have some of your own.''

His expression promptly shut down. ''Not going to happen,'' he said tightly.

''Why on earth not?''

''You know why,'' he said. ''What the hell does a man with my background know about raising a family?''

Deanna met his tormented gaze directly. ''It seems to me if anyone knows what *not* to do when it comes to raising kids, it's you,'' she said, gently but with complete conviction.

He seemed startled by her statement. ''Doesn't mean I could stick it out, any more than my folks could.''

''You're not giving yourself much credit,'' she accused.

''For good reason. Those are the genes I've got running through me.''

''You said you've been in touch with one brother recently. Does he feel the same way?''

''Pretty much,'' he said, then hesitated. ''Or at least he did.''

''What changed his mind?''

''He met someone, fell in love.''

"And got married?" Deanna guessed.

Sean nodded.

"And he's braver than you are? I doubt that," she scoffed.

"It's not about being brave," he retorted.

"Sure it is. Every marriage requires a leap of faith, even for people who don't have lousy examples all around them. The same holds true for having kids. They don't come with instruction manuals. Even the best baby books don't really prepare you for the day-in, day-out realities. But thousands—probably even millions—of people have babies for the first time every year. These parents survive, and so do the kids."

He grinned. "All this talk about bravery from a woman who didn't even want to go out on a date because the prospect scared her," he teased.

Deanna winced at the accurate accusation. "I'm not scared of dating," she muttered.

"Oh? Must be me, then. Are you scared of me, Deanna?" He stepped closer as he spoke, then reached out and traced the curve of her jaw, sending a shudder through her.

"No," she whispered, but it was evident to both of them that it was a lie. She was sure he could feel her trembling, feel the heat climbing into her cheeks.

"I want to kiss you again," he said, as if he weren't especially happy about it.

Because she had something to prove, she faced him with her jauntiest expression. "Then why don't you?" she dared him.

He rubbed his thumb across her lower lip. "You mean that?"

The truth was, she thought she might die if she

didn't feel his lips on hers in the next ten seconds. She nodded.

"Well then, I suppose it would be wrong of me to let a lady down," he said, slowly lowering his head until his mouth was a scant fraction of an inch above hers.

"Very wrong," she agreed as his lips met hers.

The explosion of need was every bit as violent and overwhelming as it had been the first time he'd kissed her. Deanna lost herself in the swirl of dark, tempting sensations, letting herself rock forward until she was crushed against him. Heat from his body surrounded her, pulling her in, making her crave more.

What on earth was she doing? This was exactly what she'd told herself to avoid at all costs. Her senses were swimming, filled with the taste and feel of Sean as he devoured her with that kiss. He shifted, and she felt the edge of the counter at her back, the hard press of his arousal against her hip. There was an odd sense of comfort in knowing that he wanted her as desperately as she wanted him, that he had as little control over his responses as she did.

"Mom! Sean!"

The sound of Kevin's shouts and the thunder of footsteps on the stairs tore them apart. Deanna barely resisted the urge to turn and splash cold water on her face before her son ran into the room. She noted that Sean deliberately turned his back to the room, dragging in deep gulps of air to steady himself before facing Kevin.

"In here," she called, her voice shaky.

Kevin raced through the door, then skidded to a stop. He studied her worriedly, then looked at Sean. "You guys aren't fighting, are you?"

"No, of course not. Why would you think that?"

"'Cause you look all funny, kinda like Hank and Ruby when they're fighting."

Now wasn't that telling? Deanna thought, resolving to ask Ruby just how much *fighting* she and Hank were doing lately. "Everything's fine," she reassured Kevin. "Did you come up here for a reason?"

"I'm starving. The other guys had to go in for dinner, so I came up to see if the burgers are ready."

"Not just yet," Sean said.

Deanna barely contained a chuckle at the gross exaggeration.

Kevin looked around the kitchen, clearly noting that the table wasn't set and that there was no evidence that dinner had even been started. "What have you guys been doing?" he asked.

"Talking," Deanna said at once. "We lost track of time."

"Oh," Kevin said, apparently placated. "Can I have a soda?"

"Sure," Sean said eagerly, reaching inside the fridge to retrieve one, then glancing at Deanna. "Okay?"

"Sure," she said. She would have given Kevin anything he'd asked for at that point, if it would have gotten him off the embarrassing topic of what she and Sean had been up to.

Kevin took his can of pop and climbed onto a chair. "What have you been talking about?" he asked, clearly settling in.

"Grown-up stuff. Nothing that would interest you, kiddo," Sean said, when Deanna remained completely mute, unable to think of a single response.

"Oh," Kevin said again, a bored expression

crossing his face. Finally he asked, "Can I watch TV?"

Sean again glanced at Deanna. She nodded. "Just until dinner's ready," she told him. "You turn it off and come when we call, okay?"

Kevin looked at the unopened package of hamburger meat sitting on the counter and rolled his eyes. "It's not like that's gonna be anytime soon, is it?"

As soon as he'd left the kitchen, Sean looked at Deanna and grinned. "Scolded by a five-year-old," he lamented. "How embarrassing is that?"

"Not as embarrassing as trying to explain what he almost walked in on," she said. "I felt as if I were sixteen again and my father caught me making out on the front porch."

He studied her with undisguised curiosity. "Did you get caught a lot?"

"Probably not nearly as much as you probably did," she said.

"Nobody much cared what I did," he said in a matter-of-fact way that said volumes about how much that still hurt.

Deanna avoided any hint of pity. "Not even the fathers of the girls you dated?"

A smile tugged at his lips, apparently at some nearly forgotten memory. "You have a point. They did care quite a lot, but I was a smooth operator. I almost never got caught kissing their precious daughters."

"Lucky you."

He winked. "Luck had nothing to do with it. I knew enough to steer clear of their front porches. I did all my kissing in the back seat of a car, blocks from home."

Deanna felt a little thrill of excitement at the image

he'd created. She wouldn't mind spending an evening in the back seat of a car with him. But given their age and experience, she doubted they'd be able to confine themselves to kissing.

"Don't even go there," Sean said.

"Where?" she asked innocently.

"I am not going to make out with you in the back seat of a car," he said firmly, his eyes twinkling and his lips struggling to hold back a grin.

She frowned at the obvious teasing. "Who asked you to?"

"Come on. You know you want to. It's written all over your face."

She shook her head and regarded him with a stern expression. "Given what you're telling me, I'm more amazed than ever that you made it to the age of twenty-nine without having at least a brush with fatherhood."

Sean's humor promptly died. "Ever heard of birth control?"

"Sure, but it's not fail proof."

"It is when I use it," he said, his expression grim.

She should have found that reassuring, but for some reason all she felt was sorrow that a man with as much parenting potential as Sean was more terrified of becoming a father than he was of walking into a blazing building.

Sean thought things had been going just great until Deanna had started pushing him about being a father. Why she couldn't see that he was a lousy candidate for such a role was beyond him. He liked kids. He got along with them. But that wasn't enough to prove that he had what it took to nurture one the way a real dad was supposed to do. Hell, he didn't know the first thing about making that kind of lifelong commitment to another human being.

He pounded the hamburgers into patties with more force than necessary, scowling as he went over their conversation in his head. He'd been honest with her, but she hadn't believed him. Like too many women Deanna apparently saw him the way she wanted him to be, not the way he was. The faith she apparently had in him was scary stuff, worse than any fire he'd ever faced.

When she'd gone into the living room to check on Kevin, he'd finally breathed a sigh of relief. He'd thrown open the window to get some air into a room that had suddenly gone claustrophobic.

A faint prickle of unease on the back of his neck told him she was back.

"You trying to tenderize that meat by pounding it to death?" she inquired lightly.

Sean stared at the hamburger patties that were less than a half inch high. "Just working in the seasonings," he claimed, molding them back into balls before flattening them on the already hot skillet.

"What can I do to help?"

"Not a thing. I've already dished up the potato salad and coleslaw. We've got tomatoes, onions, ketchup and mustard. Anything else you need?"

"Buns?" she asked, glancing around.

"In the oven warming."

"Sounds as if you have everything under control, then."

"Kevin okay?"

"He found the cartoon channel. What do you

think?'' she asked wryly. ''We don't have cable at our place.''

''That's probably a good thing. Kids spend too much time in front of TV or computers these days. They're better off outside in the fresh air, getting plenty of exercise.'' Even as the words left his mouth, he realized it was something he'd heard his foster father say on more than one occasion. Evan Forrester had obviously taught him more than Sean had realized.

''Amen to that,'' Deanna said. ''I only wish there were more places for them to play in our neighborhood. Some of the kids play in the street, but I refuse to let Kevin do that, and the nearest park's too far away.''

''Ruby could bring him here in the afternoon. There's plenty of room outside the building, and there are usually a bunch of kids out in front. I could introduce her and Kevin to some of the moms.''

''You wouldn't mind doing that?''

''Why would I?''

''It might mean you'd be bumping into Kevin more. I'm sure it's flattering to be idolized the way he idolizes you, but it can take a toll after a while. You might start to want your privacy back.''

''Dee, don't worry about it,'' he said, using the nickname he'd heard Ruby use. ''Kevin's a great kid. He's not getting on my nerves. I like having him around. And it's not as if I'm here all that much, anyway. If it'll make you feel better, have Ruby call me before they come by, to make sure it's not an inconvenience, but I can tell you right now that it won't be.''

Deanna didn't look totally convinced.

''Okay, what else is on your mind?'' he asked.

"I'm not sure it's a good idea for him to start to count on you too much," she admitted. "It's not as if you're always going to be available for him. Despite what you think now, you could eventually meet someone, get married, have your own family. Where would that leave Kevin?"

He carefully flipped a burger as he considered his response to that. "We've already discussed the likelihood that I'll never get married, so that's not an issue." He met her gaze. "Dee, I'm not going to let him down. I'll make it very clear that we're just buddies. I won't set up any false expectations."

"That all sounds very reasonable to me, but I'm an adult, not a five-year-old boy who desperately wants a dad."

Sean swallowed hard as her quietly spoken words hit home. Of course she was right to be worried. How many times as a boy had he watched with envy as his friends went off to do things with their dads? Evan Forrester had done things with him, but it had taken years before Sean had allowed himself to begin to count on his foster father really being there for him. If anything had happened to jerk the rug out from under his feet once he'd finally started to trust his foster father, it would have been devastating. Kevin had none of those defenses in place. The kid was still innocent enough to wear his heart on his sleeve.

"Would you prefer it if I steered clear of him completely?" he asked, feeling an odd sense of loss even before she replied. Though he spent time with a lot of kids, there was something about Kevin's cocky self-assurance and his vulnerability that struck a chord with Sean. Maybe he saw himself in the boy.

Deanna stood there, clearly weighing her answer for

what seemed to be an eternity before she finally shook her head. "No, that's not what I want, and I know it's not what Kevin wants. I just don't want him to get hurt."

"Sometimes it's not possible to protect the people we love from getting hurt," Sean said. "But I'll do my best not to hurt Kevin."

"I know that, or we wouldn't be having this conversation," she said. "We wouldn't even be here."

Sean tucked a finger under her chin and forced her to meet his gaze, "I'm going to do my best not to hurt you, either."

She shrugged as if her feelings were of no importance. "Yeah, well, like you said, you can't always protect people from pain. It's part of living."

"You learned that lesson from your ex?"

"Among others," she said tightly.

"Care to elaborate?"

"Not really. The important thing is that I survived." She met his gaze. "So did you."

Long after Sean had walked Deanna and Kevin back home, her words lingered in his head. He doubted she realized the significance of what she'd said. She'd managed to remind him that for most of the past decade—no, even longer than that—Sean had not only survived, he'd worked hard to keep himself safe from being hurt.

But only today had he realized that he—very much like Deanna, whether she realized it or not—had also kept himself from really living.

Chapter Seven

"What the devil is this?"

From her place at the reception desk Deanna heard the shout of the senior law partner in his office. She exchanged a glance with Ruby.

"Mr. Hodges sounds like he's on a real rampage," Deanna said in a whisper. "I wonder what it's about."

Before they could even speculate, the intercom on her desk buzzed.

"Deanna, Mr. Hodges would like to see you," Charlotte Wilson said, her tone somber. "Have Ruby cover the desk for you."

"Yes, ma'am," Deanna said, her palms sweating. She gave Ruby a shaky smile. "Pray for me."

"Don't let the man bully you," Ruby advised.

Stomach churning, Deanna walked down the corridor to the suite of offices belonging to Jordan Hodges. A glance at Charlotte's face was not encouraging. The secretary, who usually maintained a facade of icy reserve, looked as if she wanted to cry.

Deanna stepped inside the office and waited.

"Don't just stand there. Come in and close the door," her boss said, regarding her with a scowling expression.

She shut the door and crossed the room. "Is something wrong?"

"I'll say something's wrong," he said, his expression grim. "I found these papers on my desk just now." He waved an envelope in her direction. "They were supposed to be across town on the desk of opposing counsel. Care to explain why they're not?"

Deanna stared at the envelope in confusion. True, it was her job to see that the outgoing mail went out each day, but she wasn't the one who addressed it. "I have no idea. What does it say on the envelope?"

"The address label is quite clear," he said, waving it under her nose.

She snagged a corner of the envelope and studied it. Sure enough, it was addressed to a lawyer in downtown Boston. "Sir, I know I've been a little frazzled lately, but if this envelope had come across my desk addressed like this, it would have gone out," she said confidently. "It wouldn't have gotten mixed up with the incoming mail."

The color in Mr. Hodges's face had finally begun to return to normal. He sank into his chair. "It's not like you to make a mistake like this," he agreed, studying her with concern. "You say you've been frazzled. Is something wrong I should know about? Your boy's okay?"

She was surprised by the question. She rarely mentioned Kevin around the office. "Kevin's fine."

"Something else, then?"

Deanna hadn't wanted to get into her personal problems at work. She never wanted her boss to think that she had so much going on that she couldn't concentrate on her job. It was a sure way to get fired.

"It's okay," he encouraged her, pinning her with a steady gaze. "Just tell me."

No wonder the man was considered a shark in court, Deanna thought. He was relentless and he managed to cross-examine a witness with that same look of compassion on his face that he had right now. She could almost believe that he really cared about what was going on in her life.

"I really don't think there's any need for me to burden you with my problems," she said.

"Nonsense. Tell me," he said even more emphatically.

"It's just that there was this fire a couple of months ago," she said hesitantly.

"A fire? Where?"

"My building."

"How bad was it?"

"Pretty bad," she admitted, then added with some reluctance, "We lost everything."

Shock spread across his face. "Why on earth didn't you say something?"

"We've been doing okay. We're living with Ruby temporarily. I've been adding hours at Joey's to try to get enough money so we can move into our own place. To be honest, it's possible that it's catching up with me."

"You're working a second job at Joey Talifero's restaurant?" he asked, clearly shocked.

"Actually I have been for some time."

He shook his head. "Well, one thing at a time. We'll deal with your need to work a second job another time. As for the fire, why wasn't I told about it? I assume you told Charlotte."

"Actually, no." Mr. Hodges's executive secretary was the last person she would have shared her personal problems with. "I don't like to bring my problems to work. I never want you to get the idea that this job doesn't have my full attention."

He regarded her with unmistakable dismay. "Deanna, how long have you been here now? Five years, isn't it? Ever since your son was born."

She nodded.

"And every single evaluation has given you high marks for being a responsible employee, correct?"

"Yes."

"Then why on earth would you be afraid to come to me when you lose your home? I think that qualifies as the kind of thing your boss ought to know. We could help you out, give you a loan, represent you if you want to sue the landlord."

Deanna stared at him in astonishment. She had never considered asking him for free legal assistance. The kind of cases he normally handled involved hundreds of thousands of dollars, not what would amount to pocket change in his world. "You would do that?" she asked.

"Well, of course we would," he said with a hint of exasperation that she even had to ask. "What did you expect? As far as I'm concerned, every employee in this firm is like family. When anyone's having a problem, I expect them to come to me *before* it interferes with their job performance."

"Thank you. I'll remember that in the future."

"Forget the future. What about the here and now? What can I do?"

Deanna refused to ask for more money. He was already paying her a decent wage for the receptionist's job she'd been doing. And she certainly didn't want a loan she would have to struggle to pay back.

"Nothing, really. I'm handling everything."

"Not if this mistake is an example of the way you're handling things," he chided, but more gently this time. "Who was at fault for the fire?"

"The fire inspector said it was the landlord," she said. "But the landlord made it clear when I signed my lease that he wasn't responsible for damages to anything in any of the apartments, that I needed to carry my own insurance."

"Did you?"

She shook her head. "I couldn't afford it," she admitted. "And we didn't have that much. I didn't realize until we lost everything how much it would cost to replace what little we did have."

Mr. Hodges pulled out a legal pad and a pen. "What's the landlord's name?"

"Lawrence Wyatt."

To her surprise her boss reacted with disgust. "Typical of Wyatt," he muttered. "This isn't the first time I've run across him. I'll have a talk with him. I think I can promise you a settlement of some kind. Will that mean you can cut back on your hours at Joey's, maybe start getting some sleep?"

"Yes."

"See that it does," he said sternly. "And, Deanna?"

"Yes, sir."

"Next time there's a crisis, don't wait so long to come to me."

"No, sir," she said, exiting the office before the tears of gratitude stinging her eyes could fall.

Charlotte studied her worriedly. "Did he fire you?"

"No."

"Thank heaven," the secretary said fervently.

"I just can't imagine what happened, though. I'm always so careful. I know how important papers like that are."

"Mistakes happen to everyone," Charlotte said.

It was such a rare attempt at reassurance that Deanna regarded her with sudden suspicion. "You never put that envelope on my desk, did you?"

Charlotte's thin mouth remained clamped firmly shut, but the misery in her eyes was a dead giveaway.

"Never mind. I won't say anything," Deanna promised. "But you owe me, Charlotte."

The woman finally sighed. "You're right. I do. I wouldn't have let him fire you, you know. I would have confessed if it had come to that."

"But you were willing to let the mistake go on my record," Deanna reminded her. "I won't forget that."

She turned and left the suite before Charlotte could respond. When Deanna reached the outer office, she was surprised to find Sean perched on the edge of the reception desk chatting with Ruby. They both regarded her with worry when they spotted her.

"What are you doing here?" she asked Sean.

"I called him," Ruby said. "Mr. Hodges never yells like that unless he's ready to can somebody. I was afraid you were about to get fired, so I figured you'd need a big, broad shoulder to cry on. So, what happened in there?"

"He blew a gasket about a really stupid mistake, but then I explained about the fire and the extra hours at Joey's, and instead of firing me, he's going to talk to the landlord and try to wrangle a settlement for me. Actually, except for Charlotte's role in it, it's pretty amazing," she said, still bemused by the whole turn of events.

"Charlotte?" Sean asked, looking confused.

"The snake who runs Mr. Hodges's office," Ruby said, then turned to Deanna. "What did she do?"

"Turns out she was the one who made the mistake I was getting blamed for."

Ruby regarded her with indignation. "I hope you told Hodges," she said.

Deanna shook her head. "No. I didn't even realize what had really happened until after I'd left his office."

"Why the heck didn't you go right back in and tell the man the truth?" Sean demanded.

"Because it turned out okay. Charlotte won't do anything like that again."

"You're too darned noble," Ruby said.

"Actually, I'm not," Deanna said with a grin. "Now I have something I can hold over her head for years to come. Having leverage over Charlotte is a very good thing."

Ruby grinned. "Then I suggest you start by telling her you're taking the afternoon off and that she's going to cover for you. Then the three of us are going to pick up Kevin and go celebrate."

Deanna glanced at Sean to see how he was taking Ruby's attempt to plan his afternoon. He winked at her.

"Sounds like a plan to me. I don't go back on duty

till midnight." He glanced pointedly at Ruby. "Neither does Hank."

Ruby frowned at that. "So?"

"Just thought you might be interested."

"Oh, go on and call him, if you want to," Ruby told Sean grudgingly.

Deanna didn't think Ruby ought to get off the hook so easily. As Sean reached for the phone, she stopped him. "Why don't you make that call, Ruby? I'll go and speak to Charlotte."

"But—"

Deanna cut off the protest. "If I can go in there and face down dragon lady, you can call Hank."

"Oh, for heaven's sake, go. I'll call," Ruby grumbled.

She was still on the phone with Hank when Deanna came back. "How are they doing?" she asked Sean in a whisper.

He chuckled. "The subject of the celebration hasn't actually come up yet. Those two are doing a dance that defies explanation. I'm almost tempted to yank the phone out of her hand and tell the poor guy why she really called."

"She'd never forgive you," Deanna said.

"But Hank would be forever grateful. I like to shift the balance of power in our partnership arrangement from time to time."

Deanna groaned. "You men and your macho games. I thought the two of you were friends."

"We are. That's how we stay that way," he explained in a way that almost made it sound like a perfectly rational way to live.

"Whatever," Deanna said. "Thanks for coming over here when Ruby called. You didn't have to."

He laughed. ''You wouldn't say that if you'd heard her on the phone. I expected you to emerge from that office bloodied and defeated.''

''But I notice you didn't rush in to save me,'' she said.

''Only because when I got here and heard the whole story, I got a somewhat different picture of the crisis unfolding.'' He reached in his pocket and withdrew a package of tissues. ''I ran out and got these.''

''Anticipating my weeping, were you?'' she inquired, amused by his attempt at preparedness. ''A lot of men would have run at the prospect.''

He shrugged. ''Not me. I'm a sensitive kind of guy.''

''You say that as if it's a joke, but you are, you know.''

''You wouldn't say that if you knew about my plan to go in and pound your boss for making you cry in the first place.''

She bit back a smile. ''When were you going to do that?''

''As soon as I gave you the tissues and turned you over to Ruby.''

Deanna laughed. ''I don't need you fighting my battles for me.''

''I know. I can see that.''

''But I appreciate your willingness to step in, just the same.''

He seemed suddenly uncomfortable with her praise. ''Don't turn me into some kind of hero. All I did was show up.''

She reached up and touched his cheek. ''That's quite a lot for a man who claims to know nothing about sticking it out through tough times.''

"Dee—"

"Hey, you guys," Ruby interrupted. "Are we going to hang around here all afternoon or are we going to celebrate?"

Deanna met Sean's gaze and held it. "I think we have quite a few reasons to celebrate, don't you?"

For a minute she thought he might prolong the argument, but eventually he shrugged. "Whatever you say. Who am I to argue with a woman who managed to emerge from battle unscathed?"

Satisfied, Deanna turned to Ruby. "Is Hank joining us?"

Ruby shrugged. "Beats me. He was still grumbling a lot of nonsense about being awakened out of a sound sleep for no good reason when I hung up on him."

"But you did tell him where we'd be, right?" Deanna persisted.

"How could I?" Ruby asked reasonably. "I don't know where we're going to be."

Deanna sighed.

"I'll call and give him a heads-up when we get there," Sean said.

"Whatever," Ruby said, setting off down the street at a brisk pace that left Deanna and Sean trailing behind.

They stared after her, then exchanged an exasperated look.

"Do you have any idea what's going on between those two?" Deanna asked.

"Not me," Sean said.

"Well, he's your friend," she said irritably.

"And she's yours. Do you get it?"

"No," she admitted.

"Why do I think that getting in the middle of it is a very bad idea?" Sean asked.

"Because you're an intelligent man," Deanna said. "But you're going to call Hank, anyway, right?"

Sean nodded. "If only to get a firsthand look at the fireworks."

Brave man, Deanna thought. Then again, he was a firefighter. A hot, noisy skirmish probably wouldn't faze him. After all, he had lots of experience extinguishing out-of-control blazes.

Sean wasn't prepared for Hank's haggard look when he finally joined them at the ice-cream parlor that had been chosen for the celebration. He looked every bit as bad as he had a few weeks ago at the gym. He cast a sour look at Sean, barely managed a smile for Deanna, then squeezed into the booth next to Ruby, who never even looked up from her hot-fudge sundae.

Sean might not know what game those two were playing, but one thing was plain—Hank had it bad for the woman beside him. Sean couldn't think of a single occasion in the past when his pal had been so hung up on a woman. Usually after this length of time, he'd slept with a woman a few times, tired of her and moved on.

Suddenly the answer dawned on him. Hank and Ruby *hadn't* slept together. That was why they were both so cranky and out of sorts. Sean almost laughed at the irony of it. All this time, he'd been half-envious of Hank's success, and Ruby had been keeping Hank at arm's length. She was obviously a whole lot wiser than Sean had given her credit for being. He wondered if Deanna had guessed the truth, but judging from the puzzled way she was studying the two of them, she hadn't.

"Hey, Dee, feel like going for a walk?" he turned and asked her.

She regarded him blankly. "Now?"

"Seems like a good time to me," he said with a pointed glance across the table.

She looked at Ruby and Hank, then nodded with evident reluctance. "I guess so. Come on, Kevin. We're going for a walk."

Ruby's gaze shot up. "You're leaving?" she asked, a faint hint of panic in her voice.

Deanna regarded her worriedly. "Unless you want us to wait for you?"

Hank seemed to be holding his breath as he awaited Ruby's reply. She looked at him, waged some sort of internal debate that Sean couldn't interpret, then finally shook her head.

"Go ahead," she told them. "Hank hasn't even ordered yet. I can stay with him."

"You're sure you don't mind?" Deanna persisted, as Sean latched on to her hand and began tugging her from the booth.

"You heard her," Sean said. "She told us to go on."

Kevin regarded all of them with impatience. "Are we going or staying?" he grumbled.

"Going," Sean said firmly.

Deanna looked as if she might balk, but then she shrugged. "We're going."

Outside, she scowled up at Sean. "What was that all about? Why were you so anxious to get out of there?"

"Discretion," he said.

"What?" she demanded. Then understanding obviously dawned. "Oh, of course."

"You two are acting all weird again," Kevin declared with disgust.

Sean laughed. "You'll understand when you're older."

"So, where are we going?" he asked. "Is the celebration over?"

"Not yet," Sean reassured him. "How about my place? Want to head over there for a while?"

Kevin's expression immediately brightened. "Will Mark and Davey be there?"

"More than likely."

"All right!" he enthused.

"Deanna, is that okay with you?" Sean asked.

To his surprise, she looked hesitant, but one glance at Kevin's excited expression had her backing down from whatever objections she had. "Sure."

As soon as they reached Sean's apartment, Kevin spotted the older kids and took off without another word. Deanna watched him go with a contradictory mix of dismay and relief on her face. Sean wished he could read her mind.

"What's wrong?" he asked, concerned that he'd been pushing her too hard and overstepping some unspoken boundary where Kevin was concerned. He thought they'd talked that all out, but maybe she'd had second thoughts.

"Nothing, not really. I'm glad Kevin's found some friends. They don't even seem to mind that he's so much younger. It's almost as if he has big brothers. He talks about the two of them nonstop." She grinned at Sean. "Except when he's talking about you."

"There's nothing like having brothers," Sean said.

"My parents taking off was bad enough, but in some ways losing my brothers was worse. We were best buddies, especially Ryan and me. Mikey was a couple of years younger than me, four years younger than Ryan, but he trailed around after us whenever we'd let him."

"What about the twins?" Deanna asked. "You never say much about them."

"It was different with the twins," Sean recalled. "They were still practically babies when Mom and Dad left—barely two years old. From the time they came home from the hospital, Ryan and I used to take one each and feed them, first their bottles, then that yucky stuff that passes for real food." He shuddered at the memory. "If I don't ever again see another jar of mashed peas or carrots, it will be too soon. I've never seen a worse mess in my life than those two could make having lunch."

"You sure that's not the real reason you don't want to have kids of your own?" Deanna asked lightly.

"Baby food?"

She laughed. "No. I was thinking of the way babies are when you're feeding them. You realize just how dependent they are on you. It can be scary."

Sean thought back to the way he'd felt holding his baby brothers, as if he really were somebody's hero. If anything, that emotion was the one reason he could see in favor of having kids. It was all the rest—the terrifying fear of letting them down—that kept him single and childless. Instead, he'd settled for being a different kind of hero, one who never had to risk his heart, just his life.

"I suppose," he said eventually.

She seemed to sense she'd pushed him far enough. "So how's the search going for Michael?" she asked.

He shrugged, as uncomfortable with this topic as he had been with the one before. Despite how well the reunion with Ryan had gone, he had mixed feelings about the search for Michael. Most of the time he pushed it completely out of his mind. "I have no idea," he admitted. "I haven't heard from Ryan lately."

Deanna regarded him with obvious surprise. "You could always call him or stop by to see him, couldn't you? Didn't you say he owns a pub?"

"Yes, but..." He really didn't have a good explanation for why he'd been avoiding his brother. He was pretty sure it had something to do with the overwhelming feeling of happiness that had swamped him when Ryan had first come back into his life. He didn't trust that kind of emotion. It never lasted. He supposed a part of him was waiting for his brother to keep reaching out to him. Maybe he needed proof that Ryan was back in his life to stay.

Or maybe it was flat-out jealousy that Ryan had found something with Maggie that Sean wouldn't allow himself to feel.

"I'd like to go sometime," Deanna said.

He stared at her. "Go where?"

"To your brother's pub. I love Irish music. I imagine they have it there."

"On weekends," he admitted, still struggling with the fact that she'd actually initiated the idea of getting together with him.

She kept her unflinching gaze leveled on him. "Will you take me sometime?"

"What are you trying to do, Deanna?"

"Ask you on a date," she said, her expression innocent. "Wasn't I clear enough?"

He studied her suspiciously. "What if I said I'd take you to some other pub in the city?"

"Then I'd say you're avoiding your brother," she responded. "And you certainly wouldn't want me to get an idea like that, would you?"

He chuckled at the tidy trap she'd sprung. Until he'd met Deanna, he'd had no idea how many traces of cowardice lurked inside him. "No, I suppose not. I imagine you can be a real nag when you set your mind to it."

"I can," she agreed proudly. "I learned from Ruby."

Sean held up his hands in a gesture of surrender. "We'll go the first weekend I'm off," he said.

To his surprise, instead of feeling trapped, he felt a faint stirring of genuine anticipation. Maybe Ryan didn't have to be first to reach out. He'd been the one who'd searched for and found Sean, after all. And he had asked Sean to be the best man at his wedding. Maybe it was Sean's turn to take a risk and keep the lines of communication open.

He met Deanna's penetrating gaze, saw the warm approval in her eyes and realized that there could be yet another benefit to taking a tiny chink out of the wall around his heart. Eventually there just might be enough room for a woman like Deanna to squeeze through.

Chapter Eight

Joey had promised Deanna she could have Friday night off to go to Ryan's Place with Sean, but on Friday at three o'clock, he called her at the law office and said he needed her to come in after all. Deanna thought of how hard she'd had to work to get Sean to agree to go to his brother's pub in the first place and felt her heart sink.

"Joey, you can't do this to me. You promised," she said.

"I'm desperate," Joey countered. "Pauline's sick."

"What's wrong with her?" Deanna asked, instantly concerned. Joey's wife had struggled for years with diabetes. Sometimes when things got especially hectic at the restaurant, she forgot to take her insulin.

"Just a cold, but it's wiped her out. I don't want her coming in here, and she shouldn't be handling orders and sneezing all over the customers, anyway."

Deanna sighed. She could hardly argue with that. "Okay, I'll work."

"I'll make it up to you, I swear it," Joey promised. "Next week you can have the whole weekend off. Catch up on your beauty sleep."

"Next week's no good," she said at once, at least not for her plan to get Sean to visit his brother. She knew by now that Sean worked every other weekend. "I want the weekend after next. Guaranteed, okay?"

"Guaranteed. You've got it," Joey said.

"Put that in writing with a penalty clause for cancellation," she said wryly. At least thanks to working in a law office, she'd picked up a few hints about protecting her rights.

"What?" Joey asked blankly.

Deanna laughed as she imagined trying to enforce such a guarantee, even if she got Joey to sign it. "Never mind. I'll see you in an hour." As soon as she'd hung up, she drew in a deep breath, picked the phone back up and called Sean.

"I have to cancel tonight," she blurted when he picked up. "But I think you should go, anyway."

"Why do you have to cancel?" he asked, sounding suspicious. "Did you ever intend to go in the first place or was this all some scheme to make sure Ryan and I don't lose touch?"

"Of course not," she said indignantly. "I don't scheme."

"Okay then, why are you canceling at the last minute?"

Deanna had a feeling he wasn't going to be much happier about the real reason she was backing out. "I have to work at Joey's," she admitted, then added, "His wife's sick."

"And there's no one else he could call?" Sean asked, his skepticism plain. "There's at least one other waitress there that I know of."

"Adele never works weekends," she explained, referring to Joey's one other nonfamily waitress. "It's usually Pauline and me. With Pauline sick, Joey's in a bind."

"Just this once, don't you think he could have called Adele first?" Sean asked.

She saw no reason to explain why Adele always had weekends off, that she cared for an ailing husband on the days insurance wouldn't pay for a nurse. "It's not a big deal. I don't mind pitching in."

"You need time off," Sean countered. "And we had plans."

There was an odd note in his voice she couldn't interpret. "Are you more upset because I have to work or because I have to postpone our visit to the pub?"

"Both," he insisted. "I told Ryan we were going to be there, and I also know that you're stretched to the limit. You need a night off."

"Sean, you can go to the pub without me. You and your brother can spend a little time together. I'll meet him in a couple of weeks," she said reasonably.

"And the break you need? When are you going to squeeze that in?"

Deanna lost patience. "When I can," she said tightly. "Sean, my life is not one of your projects."

"I don't have projects," he said tightly, clearly exasperated. "And I don't need this."

"Well, neither do I," she retorted angrily. "I have enough on my plate without having to defend myself to you."

She hung up without listening to his response. Judging from the angry tone, it wasn't the apology he owed her, anyway.

All evening long Deanna kept expecting to look up and see Sean walk through the door. When there was no sign of him, she told herself it was for the best. She'd been running her life reasonably well for a long time now. She didn't need some man swooping in and forcing changes on her that *he* thought were for her own good.

Despite her rationalization, she was still feeling sick at heart when Joey dropped her off in front of Ruby's at ten-thirty.

"Thanks again," he said as she got out of the car. "I'm really sorry about having to call you today and ruin your plans."

"Stop apologizing. I told you it wasn't a problem."

"Then why have you spent the entire evening looking as if you lost your best friend? You and Sean had a fight about this, didn't you? I know how upset he gets over the long hours you put in."

Typical of Joey to develop insight and sensitivity when she had something she didn't want to discuss.

"I'll talk to him," Joey offered when Deanna kept silent. "I can explain."

"No, you'll stay out of it," she countered.

"But he's a good guy. I like him. So does Paulie. She'll kill me if she thinks I did anything to mess up your relationship with the guy. And since all this happened because she was out sick, she'll be even more upset."

"Sean and I don't have a relationship," she said, not entirely sure how to describe what they did have. It seemed to be evolving from day to day.

Or at least it had been. She sighed.

Joey frowned. "I really think I'd better talk to him."

"No, absolutely not. Now stop worrying and go home and check on your wife. Give her my love."

"I'll wait till you get inside," Joey insisted. "Blink the lights like always, so I'll know you're safe."

Deanna leaned down and kissed his cheek. "You are such a worrywort. Good night."

As soon as she reached Ruby's apartment, she blinked the lights, then turned and looked directly into Sean's solemn face. Her heart leaped into her throat. She wasn't entirely sure whether it was because he'd just scared the daylights out of her or because she was overjoyed to sec him. She decided to go with the fear factor.

"What on earth are you doing inside my apartment lurking in the shadows? You scared me half to death," she said.

"Sorry."

He didn't seem very sorry. "How long have you been here?" she asked.

"About an hour." He'd been sitting on the edge of the sofa, but he stood up now, took a step toward her, then stopped as if he was uncertain what to do next.

"Where's Ruby?"

"She went out with Hank. Kevin's asleep in the bedroom."

Deanna tried to process the fact that Ruby had left her son with Sean without checking with her first. Not that it was a problem, other than the fact that it was one more thing Sean could hold over her head. She recognized the reason for his knee-jerk reaction to anything he considered neglectful, but it always hurt when the accusation surfaced—spoken or unspoken.

"You're pretty high-priced for a baby-sitter. What am I paying you?"

He frowned at her attempt at levity. "Don't even go there."

Something in his tone warned her he wasn't in a joking mood. She bit back another jibe and said simply, "I'm amazed Kevin went to bed knowing you're here."

He grinned at that. "He was already asleep when I got here."

"Ah, that explains it."

He jammed his hands in his pockets in a gesture she'd come to realize meant he was uncomfortable. "So," he said, not quite meeting her gaze. "You want some coffee? I made a pot. I had a feeling it might be a long night."

"Oh?"

"I figure we've got a few things to hash out."

She studied him curiously. "Such as?"

"Why you get so uptight just because I'm concerned about you. Why I insist on acting like a horse's behind when you don't fall in with my plans."

Deanna bit back a grin. "You're right. I'll take that coffee. If we've got all that to discuss, it could be a long night."

She led the way into the kitchen, took two mugs from the cupboard and poured the coffee. "I brought home a couple of pieces of Joey's lemon meringue pie," she said, holding up a takeout box from the restaurant. "You interested?"

His expression brightened. "Sure."

Deanna set one piece in front of him but put the second piece in the refrigerator.

"You're not eating any?" he asked.

"Just a bite of yours," she said, pulling two forks out of the drawer. "I'm not that hungry. Do you mind?"

"Of course not," he said.

He leaned back and watched while she proceeded to eat most of the slice. A few minutes later Deanna stared at the empty plate with chagrin. "Why on earth didn't you stop me?"

"There's something kind of erotic about a woman with a healthy appetite," he said.

"Even when she's stealing the food off your plate?"

He leaned forward and wiped a crumb from the corner of her mouth. "Even then," he said solemnly, his gaze locked with hers. "I'm sorry, Deanna."

Her head seemed to be spinning. "For?"

"Trying to run your life. I know it's not my place, but I hate seeing what all this work is doing to you." He traced a finger under her eyes. "You're exhausted. The proof's right here."

"That's no way to lift a woman's spirits," she pointed out.

"I have to call 'em like I see 'em."

She sighed. "Sean, I realize you only take on my lifestyle because you care. I suppose I'm just not used to anyone besides Ruby caring whether I'm worn-out or not. It makes me uncomfortable."

"I can't promise to stop caring," he said, regarding her solemnly. "But I'll try to stop hassling you."

"That would be nice," she said. "And I'll try to

stop overreacting when you lose your head and do it again.''

He gave her a rueful look. "You're so sure I'll forget my promise?''

"I'm certain of it," she said. "But, oddly enough, I think that's one of the things I like best about you.''

"Care to name any of the others?''

She laughed, suddenly feeling better. "Stop fishing for compliments.''

"You know, Deanna, one of these days we're going to have to deal with the real issue between us.''

She swallowed hard at the suddenly solemn expression on his face. "What issue is that?" she asked, not entirely sure she wanted to know.

"The fact that I want you," he said simply.

Desire curled through her like the warmth of a fire on a cold winter night. She refused to let herself look away from the heat in his eyes. "I guess that's plain enough," she said, her voice unsteady despite her best efforts to seem blasé.

A smile tugged at his lips. "You're not going to admit it, are you?''

"Admit what?''

"That you want me, too.''

She drew herself up and inquired in her best imitation of a haughty princess speaking to a peasant, "Whatever gave you that idea?''

To her surprise, Sean laughed.

"Nice try, darlin', but you're not going to win any prizes for your acting.''

"I am not acting," she said irritably.

"One kiss says otherwise.''

"Are you daring me to kiss you, Sean Devaney?''

"Yep.''

"Well, you can just forget it. I don't have to prove anything to you."

"Then you don't mind if I go right on believing what I want to believe?"

She leveled a look straight at him. "Up to you. I can't control what you think."

"But you can prove me wrong," he countered mildly. "Or rather, you can try."

"That is so..." She couldn't think of a word to describe just how low she thought he'd sunk, but finally settled on the first one that came to mind. "Juvenile. That's what it is, juvenile."

He didn't seem especially offended by the accusation. In fact, he merely shrugged. "I've been called worse."

"I'm not surprised."

"Can I ask you a question?"

She studied him suspiciously. "About?"

"What the hell did your ex-husband put you through to make you so suspicious of all men?"

The question caught Deanna completely by surprise. Sean had never shown any interest in her relationship with Frankie before. And her ex-husband was not a subject she liked discussing.

"Isn't it enough that he walked out before Kevin was born and left me on my own?"

"That's pretty rotten," Sean agreed. "But I have a feeling it was more than that."

"Such as?"

"Why waste time with me speculating? I'm asking you for an explanation."

Deanna thought back to her brief marriage. She'd gone into it with stars in her eyes, convinced she was madly in love and that Frankie felt the same way.

Barely eighteen, she had defied her parents, walked away from a promised college education, given up everything and everyone to be with the charming rogue who'd stolen her heart.

But Frankie had been after more than her heart. To Deanna's everlasting embarrassment, she finally realized he'd been after her trust fund. That money was the only reason he'd been willing to make a commitment to her. After the wedding, when he'd finally understood there was no way either of them were going to get their hands on it, he'd lost interest and moved on to someone a little older, a little richer, someone whose parents hadn't disowned her.

The humiliation had been almost unbearable. There was no way Deanna could bring herself to crawl back to her parents to ask for help, which, of course, was precisely what Frankie had assumed she'd do. To this day she doubted he knew the dire straits in which he'd left her.

Despite Ruby's urging her to tell her folks what had happened and that they had a grandson, Deanna had been determined to make it entirely on her own. Though the court had awarded her child support, she'd never expected to see a dime of it, not from a man who'd expected to be supported by her family. So far she'd done a pretty lousy job of triumphing over the past, but at least she hadn't had to listen to an endless tirade of "I told you so." One day, when she was really and truly back on her feet, she would contact her parents, but not now.

In the meantime, there were all those scars, the ones that made her question her judgment, the ones that made her distrust all men. Not that anyone could possibly be after her for her money now, she thought, barely stifling a laugh.

She felt Sean's warm, steady gaze on her and finally lifted her eyes to meet his.

"Where'd you go just then?" he asked.

"Back in time," she said wearily.

"Obviously not a happy time."

"No," she said succinctly.

"Will you tell me sometime?"

"Probably not," she said.

"Because you can't talk about it?"

"That's one reason." There were others, though. She didn't want his pity, and she certainly didn't want him realizing what an idiot she was for being taken in so easily.

"Did you love him that much?" Sean asked quietly.

She had. That was the worst joke of all. She had really loved Frankie, at least the man she'd thought he was. She'd had some sort of Romeo and Juliet fantasy about the two of them defying all the obstacles in their path to live happily ever after.

"Truthfully?" she said wearily. "I didn't even know him."

Sean couldn't forget what little Deanna had revealed about her relationship with her ex-husband. Nor could he keep himself from speculating about all that she'd left unsaid. It was just one more mystery to be unraveled, one more facet to add to this fascination he couldn't seem to shake.

And despite all his promises to stop hovering over her, he couldn't seem to stop himself from worrying about the almost driven way she continued to live her life. It went beyond survival instinct. It had something to do with the past. He was sure of it.

Despite her boss's promise to help her win a settlement from her landlord, as far as Sean could see, Deanna was still working herself to death. He was damned proud of the fact that he managed to keep from butting in, hauling her home and barring the door until she got at least twenty-four straight hours of sleep. But every time he saw her, the circles under her eyes were darker, the weariness in her shoulders more evident.

Even though he'd resolved to keep silent, he couldn't stop himself from doing what he could to keep an eye on her. Something told him she was nearing the end of her rope, and he intended to be nearby whenever possible in case she needed him. What had begun as a resolution to make sure Kevin was well looked after became an obsession to do the same for Deanna.

"You know, Sean, I like Joey's food as well as the next guy, but do we have to eat there every night?" Hank inquired as they left the firehouse.

"Yes," Sean said tersely. He sighed and raked a hand through his hair as he regarded the whole group of firefighters apologetically. "Look, I really appreciate the fact that you guys are willing to go there."

"Not a problem," the others chorused. "Especially if you keep paying."

Sean winced at the reminder. He figured if Deanna found out about that, she'd be furious that he was wasting his money just to keep her under surveillance.

As the other men drifted away, Sean faced Hank. "The truth is, I'm worried about Deanna."

"Why? What's up?" Hank asked, his expression

instantly filled with genuine concern. "Her ex isn't stalking her or something, is he?"

"No. But she's tired and on edge. She can't keep up this pace forever."

"And this is your problem because?" Hank asked, though his eyes were dancing with undisguised amusement.

"Because I've made it my problem," Sean returned. "Besides, I don't know what you're complaining about. Tonight is spaghetti night. You're bound to run into Ruby."

Hank looked decidedly uncomfortable at the reminder. Sean studied him intently. "Is that a problem?"

"No," Hank said tersely.

Even though his expression warned against further questions, that didn't stop Sean from asking, "You sure about that?"

"Leave it alone, okay? My relationship with Ruby is none of your business."

"That can cut both ways, you know. I can tell you to butt out of my relationship with Deanna, as well."

Hank's laugh held little mirth. "As if you two actually have one."

Sean's gaze narrowed. "Relationships aren't just about sex, you know."

"Is that so?" Hank retorted sarcastically. "Enlighten me, then. What are they about?"

"I'm not surprised you don't know," Sean said. "Since you've always been a wham-bam kind of guy."

Hank threw up his hands. "Forget it. I ask a serious question and I get wisecracks. Who needs it?" He walked out of the station and slammed the door behind him, leaving Sean staring after him.

Well, well, well, he thought. Hank was neck deep in water and floundering. He recognized the signs because he was pretty much in over his head himself.

Sighing heavily, he went after his partner to make amends. He found Hank sitting on the running board of the fire truck, looking despondent.

"I'm sorry. I didn't realize she was really getting to you," he told Hank.

Hank scowled up at him. "I never said—"

Sean cut him off. "Save it, okay? Just save it. If you can't tell me the truth, who can you tell?"

For a minute he thought Hank might stand up and throw a punch, but he finally shrugged. "Okay, I'm falling for her," he admitted. "There. I've said it. Are you satisfied?"

Sean grinned. "It's a start."

"I don't hear you admitting that you're crazy about Deanna," Hank said sourly.

"Yeah, well, maybe I'm not as in touch with my feelings as you are."

"Like hell. Everyone around here knows you're Mr. Sensitive."

Sean laughed. "Tell that to Deanna."

"Why waste my breath? I've seen the way the woman looks at you. She already knows it."

"Actually, at the moment she thinks I'm an interfering, pushy man, and I'm not too sure which part of that she considers to be the worst crime."

"Then by all means let's get over to Joey's so you can reinforce her opinion," Hank said wryly.

"You think I should stay away, give her some space?"

"If that's what she says she wants, yes," Hank told him.

Sean considered Hank's advice. It wasn't as if he was doing anything more than satisfying his own over-protective instincts by sitting at Joey's watching Dee work.

"Maybe we should eat here at the station tonight," he said, just as a call came in for an ambulance. Though he wasn't involved in the call, he instinctively listened to the dispatcher.

He and Hank recognized the address at the precise same moment. It was Joey's.

Panic swept through Sean, even as he ran for his gear. He frowned at Hank. "You coming or not?"

"It's not our call. Let the paramedics take it."

"Are you crazy?" Sean demanded. "Get the rest of the guys. We're going over there. It could be Deanna. Or Ruby, for that matter."

"More than likely, it's one of the seniors who eat there every night," Hank said reasonably, then shrugged when Sean refused to back down. "I'll get the guys."

"I'm riding with the EMTs. I'll meet you there," Sean told him, shoving his way into the back of the departing ambulance. His scowl kept the paramedics from arguing with him.

The instant they reached the restaurant, he was bolting for the door, scanning the cluster of people gathered over someone stretched out on the floor for some sign of Deanna.

"Please, let her be in the kitchen," he muttered as he raced across the room. But something in his gut told him he wasn't going to find her in the kitchen. When Kevin wiggled through the crowd, his eyes filled with tears, Sean knew even before the boy charged at him.

He scooped Kevin into his arms. "What happened?"

"Mommy fell down," Kevin sobbed, clinging to his neck. "She won't wake up."

Sean held him tightly and rubbed his back as sobs shuddered through him. He would have given anything to put Kevin down and rush to Deanna himself, but he understood that the EMTs knew what they were doing. "It's okay. The paramedics are going to take real good care of her," he promised, saying the words aloud as much for his own benefit as for Kevin's.

When the customers recognized him, they parted, making a path so that Sean could get closer. Ruby caught his eye.

"I think she just fainted," she said, her voice tremulous, her cheeks pale. "We wouldn't have called nine-one-one except she didn't come to right away."

"Can you take Kevin for a second, so I can check on her?" Sean asked, surprised to hear the husky sound of his voice.

"Of course." She reached for Kevin. "Come here, buddy. Let Sean help your mom."

Sean sucked in a breath when he saw how pale Deanna was. Add to that the bruise already blossoming on her forehead from slamming into the floor facefirst and she looked pretty awful. He managed to find a spot next to her that wouldn't interfere with the EMTs and took her hand in his. Hers was icy cold.

"Hey, darlin', wake up," he murmured. "Let me see those pretty brown eyes of yours."

Her eyelids fluttered and a sigh seemed to wash over her.

"Come on, Deanna, you can do it," he coaxed. "Wake up."

She stirred restlessly. "No."

The word was barely a whisper, but it had him grinning. "Why not? You enjoying this Sleeping Beauty routine?"

"Not that," she said, her eyes still clamped shut.

"What then?"

"Don't want to listen to you saying you told me so."

The EMTs regarded him with a grin.

"I think she's back with us," one said. "Or at least she will be if you don't terrorize her into sinking back into oblivion."

"Her vitals are strong," another confirmed.

"You taking her to the hospital?" Sean asked.

Her eyes did snap open at that. "No," she said very firmly. "No hospital. I just fainted, for goodness sakes."

"A trip to the E.R. wouldn't hurt," Sean said, still holding her hand. "Get you checked out. Have someone take a look at that bump on your head."

Her gaze clung to his. "No hospital, please. I'm fine. See?" She started to sit up, then clutched her head and sank back.

"Whoa, darlin', how about staying real still till your head stops spinning?"

"Where's Kevin?" she asked.

"He's right here. Ruby has him."

"I need to see him. He must be scared."

Sean heard the anxiety in her voice and knew she was worried about more than Kevin's state of mind. She was worried that Sean was going to view this incident as one more example of her not being a good parent. Good parents didn't fall on their faces in front of their kids.

"Kevin's a little worried about you, but he's doing just fine. No harm done," Sean reassured her, hoping that she understood the underlying message. "Hey, Ruby, bring Kevin over here. Somebody's asking for him."

Once again Deanna struggled to sit up, this time making it with Sean's arm to prop her up. When Kevin raced toward her, she enveloped him in a hug that Sean found himself envying.

"Mom, are you okay?"

"I am now," she assured him.

Sean watched the two of them clinging to each other, and for the first time in years, he felt like an outsider again. What had ever made him think that he could fit into their tight little family circle? They had each other and that was all that seemed to matter to either of them.

The loneliness that crept through him now was even worse, somehow, than it had been years ago. He'd gotten used to it then, but lately he'd started to let himself dream. He was an idiot, no question about it.

Satisfied that Deanna was going to be fine, he stood up, took one last look at them, turned on his heel and walked away. Some people just weren't meant to have their dreams come true. It looked as if he was one of them.

Chapter Nine

Deanna was home, tucked beneath the sheets in Ruby's bed with a tray of scrambled eggs, toast, raspberry jam and tea in front of her, by six-thirty. No one had listened to her protests that she was perfectly capable of finishing out her shift. She grinned ruefully. Maybe it had something to do with Joey's liability insurance. He probably wasn't covered for waitresses fainting into people's dinners.

Ruby and Kevin sat beside the bed watching her intently, as if they weren't so sure she wasn't going to pass out again.

"Eat," Ruby finally ordered, when Deanna had yet to pick up her fork.

"I'm not hungry."

"Yeah, right. That's why you fainted, because you were so overstuffed from chowing down all day."

"Very funny," Deanna said, pushing the eggs

around on the plate. She lifted the fork to her mouth, then put it down again.

"Nice try, but you have to actually put the food in your mouth for it to do any good," Ruby commented. She studied Deanna worriedly, then glanced at Kevin. "Kiddo, I knew we forgot something. How about going into the kitchen and getting your mom a glass of juice?"

Deanna started to protest, then caught the forbidding look in Ruby's eyes and clamped her mouth shut.

As soon as Kevin was out of the room, Ruby frowned at her. "Okay, you want to tell me what's going on?"

"Nothing. I'm fine. Really."

"And I'm first lady of the United States," Ruby retorted in a tone heavily laced with sarcasm.

"Okay, it's Sean," Deanna admitted reluctantly. "He just took off. One minute he was there watching me with that worried frown on his face. The next he was gone." She noticed that Ruby didn't even try to deny that there was anything odd about Sean's behavior. Evidently she'd noticed it, too. "Did you see him go? Was he upset?"

"A woman he cares about keeled over while serving spaghetti, what do you think? Of course he was upset," Ruby retorted impatiently. "When he walked into Joey's and spotted you on the floor, I thought he was going to pass out right beside you."

Deanna recalled the gentle, coaxing tone in his voice as he'd tried to draw her back to consciousness. She also recalled something else, the quick glimpse of a totally bleak expression on his face when she was holding Kevin. Then she'd been concentrating on reassuring her son, and by the time she looked Sean's way again, he'd gone.

She was still puzzling over that memory when the doorbell rang.

"Eat your dinner while I get the door," Ruby said. "Unless it's a tall, handsome man, I'm sending whoever it is away." She regarded Deanna with a stern expression and added, "As for you, drink the juice when Kevin brings it."

"Yes, ma'am," Deanna said with a salute that mocked her drill sergeant manner.

After Ruby had gone, she toyed with the now totally unappetizing eggs, then sighed. She couldn't seem to shake the feeling that something just wasn't right about the way Sean had disappeared.

"That's no way to get back on your feet," a disapproving voice chided her.

Deanna's gaze shot to the doorway, where Sean stood regarding her uneasily.

"I'm not hungry."

"Isn't that how you landed in bed in the first place?" He crossed the room, took a look at the plate of cold, congealed eggs and dry toast, and made a face. "Give it to me."

She held tight to the tray. "Why?"

He rolled his eyes. "Do you have to argue about everything?"

"Pretty much. Otherwise, people tend to steamroll right over me."

"This could be one instance when you should let them," he said, gently disengaging her fingers and taking the tray. "I'll be right back."

She stared after him, more confused than ever. He didn't seem angry or even upset, just a little sad.

It was twenty minutes before he returned, carrying the same tray with a plate of steaming French toast with a dusting of sugar and cinnamon. He set the tray across her knees, then stood scowling down at her.

"Now, there are two ways we can do this," he said. "You can eat that like the intelligent woman we both know you are."

Deanna had to fight to hide a smile. "Or?"

He grinned, looking surprisingly eager for her to test him. "Or I feed it to you."

"I'd like to see you try," she muttered, but she picked up the fork and began to eat. After a couple of bites she stared at him in surprise. "This is really good. You made it?"

"With my own two hands," he acknowledged. "When you live on your own, you learn a thing or two about cooking or you live on frozen dinners. And at the station, we all have to take a turn at kitchen duty. Believe me, none of us are slackers. Hungry men take no prisoners."

She grinned at the image. "What else can you cook?"

"Give me a cookbook, and I'll try anything."

"You're going to make some lucky woman a wonderful husband." She'd expected the teasing remark to draw a smile, but instead, that bleak expression darkened his eyes again before he turned away to stare out the window.

"Sean?"

"Yeah?" He turned back slowly.

"Thanks for coming to Joey's tonight. I know it wasn't your call."

"No big deal."

"It was a big deal to me," she insisted. "I heard you."

He turned to face her. "What?"

"When I was still pretty much out of it, I heard your voice. I think it pulled me back to reality."

He shrugged, looking uncomfortable. "You said something like that at the time." A smile tugged at his lips. "You said that was why you wouldn't open your eyes, 'cause you didn't want to have to face me when I said I told you so."

She vaguely remembered saying that. "But you didn't say it, did you?"

"Nope. I figured you'd gotten the message anyway."

"Why did you take off without saying anything?"

"You were in good hands. You didn't need me around anymore."

Deanna heard the casually spoken words, but she was also almost certain that she heard something more, something that sounded an awful lot like pain.

"Sean?"

"Look, I've got to get out of here," he said abruptly. "I shouldn't have left the station, but I wanted to check on you." He bent down and brushed a quick kiss across her forehead. "Finish every bite of that food. If you don't, I'll hear about it."

"You've got Ruby tattling on me again?"

He grinned. "Ruby *and* Kevin. You're not going to get anything past me."

There was something oddly comforting about that, Deanna thought as she finished her meal and slowly drifted off to sleep. Not that she'd ever tell him that.

Something had changed between them, Sean concluded on his way back to the station. He couldn't quite put his finger on it, but he'd left Ruby's with the sense that he and Deanna had a new understanding. He wasn't sure yet whether that was a good thing. He wasn't crazy about the distinct possibility that she was starting to see through his defenses.

Nor was he nuts about this need he had to check up on her, to reassure himself that she was all right. Hadn't he learned anything from that moment at Joey's when he'd been an outsider looking onto the tight-knit world of Deanna and Kevin? Apparently not, because just a couple of hours later, he hadn't been able to stop himself from going back for more.

As it had turned out, he'd been right to go. Deanna evidently hadn't learned a thing from that fainting episode. She hadn't touched the food that Ruby had fixed for her. The woman needed a keeper.

Was he prepared to be that? An image of Kevin flashed through his head. If ever a boy needed a dad, it was Kevin. But he deserved one who was going to be around for the long haul. Sean wasn't convinced that he was that guy. Maybe if it were just Deanna and him, he could take that leap of faith his brother had talked about when he'd married Maggie, but not with a kid involved, a kid who didn't deserve to be let down if things didn't work out.

Sean sighed heavily. Things were getting too damned complicated. He was almost relieved when a call came in not ten minutes after he got back to the station. He dragged on his gear and headed out, eager for the distraction, eager to be doing something he knew he was good at.

Of course, a fire could be just as unpredictable as a woman, no question about that. What should have been a quick run turned into an all-nighter with two more companies involved. A fire that had started on a kitchen stove spread to nearby curtains before the old lady living there realized anything was amiss. She'd run screaming from the apartment rather than calling 911, which gave the fire a few extra minutes to blaze out of control in the old wooden structure.

"What the hell happened?" Hank muttered when they arrived to find flames shooting from several windows on the third floor. "I thought somebody's dinner caught on fire."

Sean latched on to one of the residents. "Is everybody out of the building?"

The man was clearly shaken. "I'm not sure. I just moved in last week. Second floor."

"How many apartments are there altogether?" Sean asked.

"Six, two on each floor."

"Okay, your apartment's accounted for."

"And Mrs. McGinty, it started in her place," he said. "She's right over there. And that's her third-floor neighbor with her."

"That leaves us with three more apartments we don't know about," Sean said, looking at Hank. "One on the second floor, two on the first."

He saw their lieutenant trying to get similar information from the weeping old lady and her neighbor. "What do we have, Jack?" he hollered as he hauled hoses toward the front of the building where the flames were beginning to shoot through the roof.

"Everyone's accounted for except an old man who lived on the second floor. He's hard of hearing. Neighbors tried beating on the door on their way down, but they couldn't wait. It was too hot."

"I'm on it," Sean said at once.

"You can't go in there," Jack protested. "The third floor's engulfed. It could cave in any second. You'd be trapped."

"I'm not leaving the man in there to die," Sean said, not waiting for permission before scrambling over equipment to head inside.

The heat came at him in waves, accompanied by thick smoke that blurred his vision and made him choke.

"Dammit, Sean, are you crazy?" Hank said, on his heels.

"It's one flight of steps. I can make it," he insisted, dropping down to feel his way up the stairs. "You go back."

"No way. I'm not living with guilt for the rest of my life if something happens to you while I'm standing around in the fresh air twiddling my thumbs. Now, stop arguing and move. Let's get in and out while we still can."

When Sean reached the second-floor landing, the smoke was so thick he couldn't see his hand in front of his face. He heard the crackling of flames just over head and the sizzle of the water trying to douse them.

"Come on, guys. Five minutes. Ten, tops. That's all I need," he muttered to himself. Thank God there were only two apartments. The door to the one on the right was ajar. More than likely that was the one the man outside had fled. That meant the old man was probably trapped in the apartment on the left.

He crawled across the landing, reached up and twisted the doorknob. The metal was hot to the touch, but not unbearable. No flames inside the apartment, not yet, anyway. Unfortunately, though, the door was locked.

Sean muttered a curse. "Hank, we're going to have to knock it down."

"Stand back. I'll do it. You be ready to go inside. On the count of three. Ready?"

"Ready." Sean stood up as Hank counted rapidly, then slammed his foot into the door just below the lock. It shattered on its hinges and he was inside, shouting, feeling his way through the thick smoke, coughing despite the gear meant to protect them from smoke inhalation.

He found the old man in the bedroom, next to the window. He'd passed out before he could get it open to call for help. Sean scooped him up and was about to turn around and head back the way he'd come, when wood splintered overhead and flaming beams crashed down around him, blocking his intended route of escape.

"Hank?" he shouted.

"I'm okay, but we're not going out the easy way. Open the window. I'm right behind you."

Despite the confidence of Hank's words, Sean knew his partner better than anyone on earth. He heard the faint hitch in his voice that no one else would have been able to discern.

"Dammit, Hank, what's wrong? Now's no time to lie to me!"

"Just get out of here," Hank shouted back.

He wasn't nearly as close as Sean would have liked. He put the old man down long enough to get the window open. In seconds there was a ladder against the side of the building, and he was able to hand the victim to one of the other firefighters. Still there was no sign of Hank.

Sean looked back through the flames, wincing at the sting of smoke that blurred his vision. Hank was on the far side of the burning beam, on the floor, not moving. Sean had to fight against the wave of panic that crawled up his spine. He was not leaving Hank in here to die, and that was that.

He met the gaze of the firefighter at the top of the ladder. "I'm going back for Hank."

"Dammit, Devaney, there's no time."

"I want you out of there now," the lieutenant shouted up at him.

"No way in hell am I leaving Hank in here." He glanced at the firefighter at the top of the ladder. "Move it. Buy me some time. Two minutes. That's all I need."

The man seemed about to argue, but then he was moving, shouting at the firefighters down below. Water began to splatter down through the destroyed roof. Flames sizzled and sputtered, but didn't die. The smoke grew even thicker and more acrid, the way a doused campfire did just before it died out.

Sean dodged another falling beam engulfed with flames to reach Hank's side. He didn't waste time on questions about his friend's injuries. Hell, he wasn't even sure if Hank was conscious. Sean just picked Hank up as if he weighed nothing and pushed his way back toward the window, oblivious to the heat, just totally focused on getting his partner to safety.

He handed Hank's limp body through the window to another waiting firefighter, then crawled out behind them. On the top rung, he ripped off his gear and sucked in a lungful of fresh air, coughed, then gasped for more.

Not until he was on solid ground again did the rush of adrenaline fade. He barely made it to where the paramedics were working on Hank before collapsing.

"He going to be okay?" Sean demanded, his voice hoarse.

"Looks as if he might have broken an ankle," Cal Watkins replied. "Smoke inhalation, too, but he'll make it." He looked over at Sean. "What about you?"

"I'm fine," Sean insisted.

Cal frowned at him. "Yeah, you sound fine, like you've been smoking for about a hundred years and have no lung capacity left." He slapped an oxygen mask over Sean's face, then peered at him more intently. "A couple of minor burns on that handsome face, too. Don't worry, though, they'll just give you a little character. You can hitch a ride to the hospital in the same ambulance with Hank."

Sean hadn't even felt the burns. Now, though, with the adrenaline wearing off and relief coursing through him that Hank was going to be okay, he was beginning to feel the pain. It wasn't the knock-you-on-your-butt pain some of the other guys had described after burn injuries, but it was bad enough to keep him from arguing about the ride to the hospital. Besides, one glance at his lieutenant's fierce expression told him he'd be better off in the emergency room than facing the storm that was brewing over his decision to go into that burning structure not just once, but twice, in direct defiance of orders.

Thanks to plenty of repeat visits to various fallen firefighters, Sean had a passing acquaintance with most of the burn specialists at the hospital. It was the first time, though, that he'd been on the receiving end of their attention. They were like a bunch of mother hens. He kept explaining that he could go home, but before he knew it he was upstairs in a room with a grumbling Hank in the bed next to his and a male nurse who looked like a linebacker for the New England Patriots stationed at the door.

He tried the phone, but calls were blocked. He turned to the nurse. "I don't suppose you could get this phone turned on, could you?" he asked. He really needed to call Ryan in case word leaked out about his injuries. He debated a call to Deanna, but decided it could wait until after daybreak. She needed her sleep.

"I'll have a phone hooked up in here in the morning," the nurse said.

Sean tried his best smile. "It's almost morning now. What difference will a couple of hours make?"

"The orders are on your chart. No calls. No visitors till morning. You both need some rest."

"What about the old man we pulled out of that building? How's he doing?"

The nurse shrugged. "Haven't heard."

"Couldn't you find out?" he coaxed. "After all, we risked our lives to save him. I'd sleep better knowing he's going to be okay."

The man scowled, but finally relented. "I'll check. You stay put."

As soon as he was gone, Sean slid out of bed, cursing the indignity of the hospital gown that was flapping around him. He made it as far as the door, opened it and peeked out, when a familiar scent caught his attention. He looked up straight into Deanna's worried face. Ruby was right on her heels.

"Going somewhere?" Deanna inquired lightly.

"Looking for a phone that works," he admitted, surprised by how glad he was to see her.

"Not to call me, though, right? It wouldn't occur to you that Ruby and I might hear about the fire and panic."

He frowned at her tone. She was clearly angry. "It's not morning yet. The local news isn't on, and I doubt this fire was big enough to make CNN."

"Actually, your boss called because Hank asked him to," Ruby said. "He also tried to let Ryan know you were here."

Sean didn't even try to hide his shock. "The lieutenant called you and my brother?"

"That's the one," Deanna said. "Nice man. Seems to understand the importance of keeping friends and family informed."

"Of course, the staff has kept us cooling our heels out here in the hall," Ruby complained. "But now that you've tried to make a break for it, I figure we can come inside and prevent any more attempted escapes. Out of my way, handsome. I need to see for myself that Hank's in one piece."

She pushed past Sean and left him standing there to face a still-indignant Deanna.

"I would have let you know what happened," he swore. "You weren't in great shape yourself last night. I didn't want to worry you."

"Nice try, but I'm not buying it. Who were you about to call? And don't try to pretend it was me."

"Ryan, actually."

She nodded. "Good choice. Give me the number. I'll try him again. I'll tell him to come by in a couple of hours after you've had some sleep."

For a woman who'd collapsed herself not twelve hours earlier, she sounded amazingly strong. And she didn't seem inclined to take no for an answer. Sean didn't know quite what to make of this new, take-charge woman who was facing him down. This woman didn't look as if she needed anyone to rescue her. She looked more like an avenging angel herself.

"Where's Kevin?" he asked.

"Asleep in the waiting room right over there."

"Take him home. As you can see for yourself, I'm fine."

She reached up as if to touch his face, then pulled back, her eyes filling with unexpected tears. "Yeah, I can see that."

"Surface burns," he said, clasping her hand and pressing a kiss to her knuckles. "They'll heal before you know it."

"It could have been worse," she said with a shudder.

"But it wasn't."

"I heard the whole story. The lieutenant's mad as hell, but he said you saved two lives tonight—Hank's and the old man's."

Sean sighed with relief. "He's going to make it, then. I just sent the nurse out to check."

"Yeah, sure. You sent the nurse out so you could make a break for it."

He grinned. "That, too."

"I thought you said Hank was the danger junkie," Deanna said, her frown back in place. "But the lieutenant says you're the one who took all the chances tonight."

"Calculated risks," Sean insisted. "There's a difference." To his chagrin, the night's events finally caught up with him and his knees almost gave way. He reached for the doorjamb, but Deanna was right there, putting his arm around her shoulder and leading him back into the room, muttering a stream of surprisingly colorful curses all the way. He grinned.

"I hope you don't use that language around Kevin," he said.

"Of course not." She scowled at him. "He never deserves it."

"And I do?"

She settled him onto his bed and pulled up the sheet as if she were tucking in her son. This time when she reached out to Sean, she did touch him, smoothing his hair gently back from his forehead.

"Yes," she said softly. "I think you do."

Sean sighed, relaxing at last. He let his eyes drift shut.

"Not supposed to be this way," he murmured. "Supposed to be looking out for you."

"Oh, Sean, don't you realize you have people who care about you now?" Deanna whispered. "People who would be devastated if anything happened to you?"

Her fierce words drifted into his subconscious and he finally fell asleep, a smile on his lips.

Chapter Ten

Despite assurances that Sean was going to be fine and that he'd probably be released from the hospital by midday, Deanna refused to budge from his bedside. Ruby was just as adamant about staying beside Hank. Deanna left the room only long enough to get her son. Kevin crept in from the waiting room, studied Sean intently as if to satisfy himself that his hero was okay, then fell back to sleep in a chair in the corner.

Deanna had never in her life been as terrified as she had been the night before when the lieutenant had called to inform Ruby about the fire. Nor had she ever seen Ruby as shaken. Despite the lieutenant's reassurances that both men were going to make it, neither Ruby or Deanna had hesitated before dragging on clothes and heading for the hospital to see the men for themselves.

"I've never felt this wiped out in my life," Ruby mumbled from across the room.

"It's been a long night. We should probably go home, shower and go to work," Deanna said half-heartedly.

Ruby looked at her as if she were crazy. "I'm not going anywhere. Give me some change. I'll call the office and explain things to Charlotte the snake."

Deanna managed a weak grin at the venomous but fitting nickname. "You really need to stop calling her that. One of these days you're going to say it in front of her."

"Well, she is a snake," Ruby retorted. "Just look what she did to you, making you take the rap for that report that didn't get mailed to the other law firm. I guarantee she'll never own up to that to Hodges."

"She's been better since then," Deanna said. "Haven't you noticed? She actually says good morning when she comes in, and adds please and thank you to her commands."

"Only because she's terrified you're going to rat her out to Hodges," Ruby insisted.

"Hey, ladies, could you keep it down? My head's killing me," Hank muttered hoarsely.

Ruby was on her feet in an instant, the expression on her face a dead giveaway. Deanna wondered if Hank could see it. Was he smart enough to see all the love Ruby would willingly shower on him, if only he was ready for it?

"Hey, beautiful."

Sean's voice drew Deanna's attention away from the other couple. She smiled at him. "Now I know your injuries were more severe than they're saying, if you think I'm beautiful."

"You are beautiful." He started to sit up, then winced and fell back down. "Have you been here all night?"

"Yes."

"Kevin?"

She gestured toward the corner. "Sound asleep."

"Go home."

"Trying to get rid of me after I've invested all this time and energy worrying about you?" she teased.

"You fainted last night. You need to be in bed, too." A devilish grin crept over his face. He patted the bed beside him. "Of course, there's plenty of room here."

Deanna laughed. "I don't think so. By the way, after you fell asleep I tried to reach your brother. There was no answer at the apartment, so I left a message on the answering machine at the pub. Somebody named Rory called here a little while ago and spoke to the nurse. He says Ryan and Maggie went away for a couple of days, but they'll be back this afternoon and he'll let them know what happened."

"Thanks." He glanced across the room toward Hank. "Hey, buddy, how are you feeling?"

Hank's pithy response had them all grinning.

"Watch your language," Sean said, sobering. "Kevin's here."

Hank winced. "Sorry." He fell silent, his expression unreadable. "Hey, buddy, I owe you."

"You don't owe me anything," Sean said. "You'd have done the same for me."

"Doesn't change the fact that you risked your life to come back after me."

"I'm the one responsible for you being in that

building in the first place. If I hadn't been so damned stubborn, you'd never have been in danger.''

Deanna heard the unmistakable regret in Sean's voice and knew that he'd have been tormented for the rest of his life if he hadn't gotten Hank out alive. She reached for his hand and squeezed.

''Just be grateful you're both here to tell the tale,'' she said. ''You can't go back and change the past.''

Sean studied her intently. ''Something you might want to remember, as well,'' he said lightly.

Before she could reply, Kevin yawned widely, blinked and stared around the room until his gaze fell on Sean.

''Hey, Sean,'' he said sleepily.

''Hey, kiddo.''

Wearing socks but no sneakers, Kevin padded over to the side of the bed, his gaze immediately drawn to Sean's injured face. ''Does that hurt?''

''Not too much.''

Kevin nodded, his expression thoughtful. ''Still, I'm thinking maybe I don't want to be a firefighter after all. You can get hurt real bad.''

''Knocked off your pedestal already,'' Hank teased Sean.

Deanna saw a flicker of sorrow in Sean's eyes, but he managed a grin. ''You've got a lot of years before you have to decide what you want to be,'' she told her son.

''Maybe it would be cool to be a doctor,'' Kevin said.

Ruby grinned at him. ''Then you'd have to give shots,'' she teased.

Hank moaned. ''Don't go talking about shots, okay?''

Kevin's eyes blinked wide at the evident hint of panic in Hank's voice. Ruby and Deanna both stared at him, as Sean began to chuckle.

"Don't tell me you're scared of shots," Ruby said to Hank, apparently delighted by the evidence that the courageous firefighter had a very human weakness.

"What if I am?" he retorted defensively. "A healthy respect for needles seems like a perfectly normal reaction to me."

The same nurse who'd been on guard duty during the night appeared just then and overheard Hank's remark. "Uh-oh, don't tell me I'm going to need restraints for this."

Hank frowned at him. "Who the hell are you?"

"Our warden," Sean said grimly. "I remember him from when we first came in. And judging from that tray he's carrying, he's armed."

Ruby leaned down until her face was scant inches from Hank's. "Concentrate on me. I promise you won't feel a thing," she said, then glanced up to wink at the nurse.

Hank opened his mouth to protest, but Ruby swooped in and kissed him just as the nurse administered the shot. Deanna glanced at Sean and saw the speculative gleam in his eyes as the nurse headed his way.

"Forget it," she told him.

"What?"

"You're a big boy. Take your shot like a man."

Kevin frowned at her. "But, Mom, can't you at least kiss it and make it better?"

"Yeah, Deanna, that's not too much to ask, is it?" Sean coaxed. He bravely held out his arm for the shot, but kept his gaze locked with Deanna's.

"Oh, for heaven's sake," she muttered, after the nurse had finished. She bent down to press a kiss to Sean's arm. She doubted he'd felt a thing. "Better?"

She stared into eyes twinkling with pure mischief.

"Not yet, but I think I'm getting there." He tapped his lips. "How about another one right here?"

She planted her hands on her hips and frowned at him. "Did something happen to your mouth?"

"It hurts real bad," he assured her.

"Liar," she accused, but she was laughing. And oh, so tempted.

"Really, really bad."

Knowing that the room was filled with avid spectators, she had two choices. She could ignore the teasing, plaintive note in his voice and walk right out of the room and wind up labeled as a coward. Or she could kiss him and let the man jumble her senses one more time. It was a no-brainer.

Deanna stepped closer, locked her gaze with his and bent down, stopping just as his lips parted and his breath caught. Let him wonder, she thought. Let him feel that edgy sense of anticipation that he triggered in her.

But before he could wonder or feel much of anything, his hand circled the back of her neck and drew her down until their lips met. The teasing kiss she'd intended got lost in yet another swirl of wild sensations and drugging heat.

Apparently, though, Sean was as aware as she of their audience, because he released her mere seconds after claiming her mouth. As she braced herself on the side of the bed and tried to regain her composure, he winked at her.

"I'm feeling better already," he announced cheer-fully. "How about you?"

She leaned close and whispered for his ears only, "I'm feeling an almost overwhelming need to make you pay for that."

His laugh echoed in the room. "I can hardly wait."

Sean was going stir-crazy. The doctors had refused to release Hank, so even though they'd released Sean around noon, he was sticking close to make sure his partner didn't do anything foolish. He'd finally con-vinced Ruby, Deanna and Kevin to go home for some sleep, so there was no one to talk to except a man who growled the few responses he deigned to make. Ob-viously, as far as Hank was concerned, Sean was a traitor for not helping him to make a break for it.

The day nurse was a pretty young woman named Susie, a vast improvement over the scowling, muscular night nurse. In the past Sean would have wandered down to the nurses' station and flirted with her to kill some time, but images of Deanna kept him in the chair beside Hank's bed.

He was about to go down to the gift shop in search of some magazines, maybe even a decent book, when the door opened and Lieutenant Beatty walked in.

"Good. You're still here," he said to Sean, then nodded toward the sleeping Hank. "How is he?"

"Cranky but on the mend," Sean said.

"I heard that," Hank retorted, cracking one eye open. "Hey, Lieutenant, how's it going?"

Their boss dragged over a chair, then looked from one to the other with a grim expression. "Here's the thing," he began in a tone that sent a chill up Sean's spine. "There's a school of thought that the two of you deserve medals for bravery for going into that building and getting that old man out safely. If it were up to the mayor, there'd be a damned ticker tape parade.''

Sean knew it wasn't up to the mayor. It was up to the fire chief and this man, and the lieutenant definitely did not look as if he wanted to hand out any medals.

''What's the other option?''

''Suspension for defying not one but two direct orders.''

Sean winced. ''I think I see where this is going, but I've got to tell you, if I had it to do over again, there's nothing I would have done any differently.''

''Same here,'' Hank said loyally.

The lieutenant's scowl deepened. ''Couldn't you show even the tiniest hint of remorse? Give me something to work with, guys. You're two of the best men I've got. I don't want to put you out on unpaid leave.''

Sean's gaze narrowed. ''You don't?''

''Not if I can help it, but chain of command and discipline are essential. I can't have rogue firefighters making decisions that put their lives or the lives of others at risk. If you two had gotten yourselves killed in that fire, the buck would have stopped with me. I was the highest-ranking officer on the scene.''

Sean knew he was right. Jack Beatty was a career firefighter who'd risen through the ranks, a man who took his responsibilities seriously. He'd made a tough call under extreme pressure. That Sean's instincts had been right was almost beside the point. He could just as easily have been wrong, and three people could have died inside that burning building.

''I couldn't let that old man die in there, not when there was a chance I could save him,'' Sean said, then held up his hand when the lieutenant seemed about to argue. "However, I see your point. It wasn't my call to make."

"And next time you'll listen to the officer in charge," the lieutenant coaxed.

"And next time I'll try to listen to the officer in charge, before doing something on my own," Sean said.

Jack uttered a resigned sigh. "Close enough. I'll speak to the mayor. You can have your medals, but he can forget the parade."

"Was he really talking about a parade?" Hank asked.

Sean frowned at him. "Be grateful we're not sitting on our butts doing nothing for a month."

Hank glanced pointedly at the cast on his ankle. "I'm pretty certain I'm going to be sitting on mine, even though Jack, here, has let us off the hook."

"Yes, but you'll still have a paycheck," Sean pointed out. "If you're smart, you'll talk Ruby into going to some romantic seaside cottage while you recuperate."

"You've got plenty of vacation time coming," the lieutenant pointed out to Sean. "You could take a break, too. I know how you hate working with anyone besides Hank, because the other men actually listen to what I tell them to do."

Sean tried to imagine a week on Cape Cod with Deanna and Kevin. The idea held tremendous appeal, but he doubted he could get her to go for it...unless Hank and Ruby went, as well. Maybe they could convince the women this was a real mission of mercy.

"I'll think about it," he told the lieutenant. "And thanks for letting us off the hook this time."

"Self-preservation," Jack said. "Can you imagine the outcry if two men who'd saved an old man's life ended up suspended?" He patted Hank's shoulder, then shook Sean's hand. "You two try to stay out of trouble, okay?"

"We always do," Hank said solemnly.

The lieutenant shook his head. "If only that were true."

After he'd gone, Sean felt Hank's gaze studying him. "What?"

"You've got something going on in that head of yours. Care to tell me about it?"

"I was thinking about Cape Cod," he admitted. "The five of us out there for a week. I could call a couple of people, see if there's a house available. What do you think?"

Hank's expression grew thoughtful. "I suppose Ruby might go for it, if you guys came along."

"I was thinking the same about Deanna. She'll only say yes if you and Ruby agree and we play the pity card, tell 'em we need to recuperate from our ordeal."

"It won't exactly be a romantic getaway with all of us under one roof," Hank said. "But that's a good thing, right? Keeps things from getting too serious."

"Right," Sean agreed, warming to the idea. "I'm thinking a big house, lots of bedrooms."

Hank grinned. "And if some of them don't happen to get used, well, that's just too bad."

"Hey, watch it," Sean chided. "There will be a kid present."

"I'm injured," Hank said pitifully. "Let me dream."

Sean laughed. "Okay, you dream. I'm going to make some calls. Then we can talk to Ruby and

Deanna. You should probably go first. If you can sell Ruby on the idea, she'll help with Deanna."

"Use the kid," Hank recommended. "You talk Kevin into a week at the beach, his mother will never say no."

"That would be sneaky and underhanded," Sean retorted, then sighed. "I'll only use it if I have to."

This trip was going to be perfect. He was going to get a little quality time with Deanna, Kevin was going to get a real vacation at the beach, and Deanna was going to get some much needed R and R. And all of it in the guise of keeping poor, injured Hank company. How noble and selfless was that?

Deanna listened to Sean's entire pitch with a perfectly straight face. It sounded good, noble even. A week on Cape Cod keeping Hank from going completely bonkers while his broken ankle began to heal. Ruby had even bought into the scheme.

"But I'll only go if you will," she'd told Deanna not ten seconds ago.

Now Ruby and Sean sat side by side awaiting Deanna's decision.

"And this is all about Hank?" Deanna asked, her gaze on Sean's face.

"Absolutely," he said. "Taking time off is hard on him, especially when he can't get around all that well. Hank's an active guy. Forced immobility will make him impossible to live with."

She grinned. "So you want us around to be a distraction for an incredibly cranky man? Sounds like fun."

"Oh, I think I can guarantee his mood will improve with you ladies underfoot, Ruby especially."

"Charlotte will have a cow if the two of us ask for vacation at the same time," Deanna said to Ruby. "You know she counts on you to fill in for me if I so much as go to the ladies' room."

"She can hire a temp," Ruby countered. "The firm can afford it. Hodges has won two huge settlements in the past week."

"Not to change the subject, but speaking of settlements," Sean said to Deanna, "what's he done for you lately? Has he managed to get you a dime from that irresponsible landlord of yours?"

Deanna thought back to the conversation she'd had with her boss just two days ago. She'd kept the news to herself, because she could hardly believe it was going to happen. "He settled," she confessed. "The check's supposedly in the mail."

Ruby whooped and ran over to give her a hug. "Way to go, Dee! How much?"

"Not a fortune," she said, trying to caution Ruby against getting too excited. "But five thousand dollars will go a long way toward getting Kevin and me a place of our own and a little bit of furniture."

"Is Hodges taking a cut?" Sean asked suspiciously.

She shook her head. "Not a dime. I offered, but he said I deserved a lot more, so he wasn't taking any of it."

"Well, well, well, a lawyer with a conscience. I'm impressed," Sean said.

"Don't be," Ruby said wryly. "All he did was make a couple of threatening phone calls to the guy. He didn't even waste any corporate stationery."

"Well, whatever he did, it worked and I'm grateful," Deanna said. She looked at Sean. "So your timing couldn't be better, actually. I was thinking that

Kevin deserved a vacation before summer's completely over, and that I'd use a little of this money to pay for a couple of days at the beach.''

Sean's expression brightened. ''You're saying yes?''

''Yes,'' she said, unwilling to think about the prospect of spending several lazy nights in Sean's company on a romantic, moonlit beach. ''But we're chipping in for part of the expenses.''

''Absolutely not,'' Sean said, his jaw set stubbornly.

''Absolutely yes,'' Deanna said just as firmly.

''Can we dicker over the finances later?'' Ruby begged. ''I want to go tell Hank.''

''Go,'' Sean and Deanna said in unison.

Sean chuckled. ''I think we can finish this discussion without bloodshed.''

Deanna frowned at him. ''Don't count on it.''

Ruby shook her head. ''Can you two play nice, or do I need to send Kevin in here to referee?''

''We're two civilized adults. We'll be fine,'' Sean reassured her.

''One of us is civilized. The other one is stubborn as a mule,'' Deanna countered.

When Ruby had gone, Sean met Deanna's gaze. ''I'm glad you said yes.''

Her heart flipped over in her chest at the heat that rose in his eyes. ''Sean, we're not going to be alone out there.''

''I know that, but I imagine we can steal a few minutes to ourselves from time to time.''

''To do what?''

He drew her to her feet and into his arms. ''This,'' he murmured, kissing her until her toes curled.

''And no more,'' she said in a shaky voice.

"And no more," he agreed solemnly, then grinned. "At least not the first night."

Anticipation shot through her, tempered only by a stern reminder that this was going to be essentially a family vacation with lots of people under that same roof. Sean would never pressure her into turning it into something else, not with Kevin just down the hall.

But he might tempt her, she thought, glancing into his eyes. They were sparkling with pure mischief. Oh, yes, he was definitely going to tempt her. And she was going to have to draw on an already overtaxed reserve of willpower to resist. Heaven help her! It was going to be a really, really long and dangerous week.

Chapter Eleven

The house in Truro was covered in soft-gray shingles that had been weathered by countless storms. The shutters were white, and window boxes full of bright flowers hung on the railing around the porch. The house was within sight of the beach dunes, and, with the windows open, a salty breeze wafted through the bright, cheerful rooms. Deanna had never seen such a lovely place. It reminded her of a house her parents had rented years ago at the Jersey shore, but this one was smaller, cozier.

"Hey, what was that look about?" Sean asked, regarding her with concern. "You looked so sad all of a sudden."

She forced a smile. "Just thinking about a time long ago and far away."

"Did it involve Kevin's father?" he asked.

She heard the tension in his voice and quickly reassured him. "Absolutely not. Frankie and I never went on a vacation."

"Your parents, then?"

She sighed at the accurate guess. "Yes."

"You don't say much about them. Are they dead?"

"To me," she said softly, unable to stop the tears that welled up in her eyes. She'd told herself a thousand times that what had happened years ago didn't matter, but there was an ache in her heart that never seemed to go away.

Sean frowned. "What does that mean?"

"They didn't approve of me marrying Frankie. We haven't spoken since," she said, giving him the short, unemotional version that omitted all of the rage and accusations that had left her feeling raw and anguished on the day she had walked out of their house for the last time. The fact that their concerns had been well-grounded was something she still hated to admit.

Sean regarded her with surprise. "You never told them he'd left you?"

She shook her head. "At first I kept silent because I didn't think I could bear to hear them gloat over having been right about him. Then it became a matter of pride. I didn't want to go to them when I needed help."

"Do they know about Kevin?"

"No."

She saw the war of emotions on Sean's face. "You realize who's hurt most by that, don't you?"

She refused to acknowledge that her son could be hurt by the absence of two people he'd never even known.

"Deanna, you need to contact them," Sean said. "Give them another chance."

She leveled a look straight into his eyes. "The same way you've given *your* parents a second chance?"

Sean winced at the comparison and his jaw set. "It's not the same thing," he insisted. "I don't even know where my parents are."

"One of these days you will. Ryan's determined to find the whole family, isn't he? What will you do then?"

"We're not discussing my family," he said tightly, "we're talking about yours. Kevin ought to have a chance to know his grandparents and vice versa."

"You're setting a double standard, and you know it," she accused, hurt that he, of all people, didn't understand why she might never want to see her parents again. They'd made the decision to turn their backs on her. She'd asked nothing from them but their love, and they'd withheld it. How was that any better than what his parents had done?

Hurling the one comment guaranteed to infuriate him, she said, "Besides, this is none of your business."

With that she whirled around, shouted for Kevin and headed for the beach at a brisk pace. She wasn't surprised when Sean didn't bother to follow. After all, she'd just slammed a door very firmly right in his face.

Sean had had no idea that he and Deanna had so much in common. Granted the break with her parents had come when she'd been an adult, and she'd made her own choice about it, choosing Frankie Blackwell over her family, but the fact was, they were both facing a future without the people who had given them life. If he wasn't anxious to change that in his own situation, why was he so insistent that Deanna should

be? Was it because he wanted for her—for Kevin—
what he wasn't willing to fight for for himself?

He heard the thump of Hank's cane hitting the
porch, but he refused to turn around. He wasn't sure
how much his friend had overheard, but knowing
Hank, it had been enough to ensure that he'd have an
opinion to offer. Probably one Sean had no desire to
hear.

"It's going to be a long week, if you don't go after
her and apologize," Hank said, coming up to lean on
the railing next to him.

"Why should I be the one apologizing?" Sean
grumbled, even though he knew the answer as well as
Hank did.

Hank grinned. "Maybe because she's right. You set
impossibly high standards for everyone else when it
comes to family, but you don't exactly apply the same
rules to yourself. How many times have you even seen
Ryan since you were best man at his wedding?"

"We're both busy," Sean said defensively.

"The man owns a pub," Hank retorted. "You know
where to find him any night of the week."

Sean had no argument for that. "Deanna just took
me by surprise. I had no idea that she was on the outs
with her family. I assumed she didn't have any, since
she'd never mentioned them."

"You don't mention yours, but they're out there,"
Hank reminded him.

Sean scowled at him. "You are so damned annoying when you find a chink in my armor."

Hank grinned. "We live to serve. Go after her. I
don't think I can stand an entire week of you two
dancing around each other. Besides, it'll ruin the romantic vibes."

Sean glanced pointedly toward the door. "Speaking of romantic vibes, where is Ruby?"

"Hiding in her room," Hank said. "Upstairs. She refused to take the one next door to mine on the first floor. She left it for you."

"Sorry."

"Me, too. The thought of looking up into your ugly mug if I call out in the middle of the night is not exactly the scenario I envisioned when we came out here." His expression brightened. "But I'm confident I can get her to change her mind eventually. I'm impossible to resist when I really put my mind to it."

Sean studied him curiously. "Is this just about sex? Is that all you were hoping for this week?"

Hank shrugged, looking more at a loss than Sean had ever seen him. "Hell if I know. That woman has more excuses for keeping me at arm's length than any female I ever met."

Sean chuckled at the confirmation that Ruby wasn't sleeping with Hank. "She still has your undivided attention, though, doesn't she? In my book, that makes her the smartest woman you've ever dated."

Hank didn't seem impressed by his analysis.

"What about you and Deanna? Anything going on?"

Sean wasn't particularly happy at having the tables turned on him. "No," he said succinctly. "Mutual decision."

"Yeah, right," Hank said skeptically. "If it's mutual, it's only because you're scared. Are you finally in over your head?"

Sean thought about the feelings that welled up in him every time Deanna walked into a room. Some were familiar—attraction, heat, lust. And some were emotions that usually sent him racing in the opposite direction—vulnerability, protectiveness, a longing for the kind of future he'd never allowed himself to imagine before.

"Getting there," Sean admitted aloud for the first time. He sighed heavily. "Guess I'd better go find her and apologize."

"If you want to do it right, you can always send Kevin back up here. Ruby will be glad of the chaperon."

Sean laughed. "Poor kid. He has no idea the heavy burden he's carrying on his shoulders this week."

"Probably best to keep it that way," Hank said. "Or you'll have something else you'll need to apologize to Deanna for."

"I think there's enough crow on my plate for now," Sean said, then headed off to get his first taste of it.

He found Deanna walking along the beach, shoulders slumped, hands tucked in the pockets of her light windbreaker. Kevin was running head of her, ducking in and out of waves as they splashed against the shore. The look on his face was one of pure joy. Whatever else came out of this week, Sean was glad he'd been a part of giving the boy this happy memory. As a kid, he'd always managed to get sick on the day everyone in school was supposed to talk about their summer vacation. He'd hated that he never had anything to talk about while everyone else shared stories about their weeks at camp or trips to the beach, to ball games or amusement parks.

Kevin looked up, spotted Sean and gave a shout, then began racing toward him. Sean saw Deanna's shoulders stiffen perceptibly, but she stopped and turned to wait for Sean. Even if she wasn't quite literally coming back to meet him halfway, it was something. He had to give her credit for not backing down from the encounter.

"I'm sorry," Sean mouthed silently as he scooped Kevin high in the air and perched the boy on his shoulders.

Deanna's serious expression didn't acknowledge the apology, but some of the tension seemed to drain out of her.

"How's the water?" he asked.

"Cold," she said, just as Kevin shouted, "It's great! Can we go swimming?"

Sean looked to Deanna.

"I'm not going in there," she said with a shiver.

Sean laughed. "Then I guess it's just you and me, buddy. You wearing your suit?"

"No," Kevin said, clearly disappointed.

"Run on up to the house and change, then," Sean said. "Your mom and I will wait right here."

A flicker of dismay crossed Deanna's face, but she didn't argue.

After Kevin had gone, Sean repeated his apology, trying to explain his attitude toward his own family, an attitude he admittedly tried never to examine too closely.

"I know your heart's in the right place, that you're thinking about Kevin," Deanna conceded when he finished. "But when it comes to my folks, you don't know what you're talking about."

"I know."

"Then you'll drop it?"

"If it will wipe that frown off your face, yes."

A smile trembled at the corners of her mouth.

Sean reached over and touched a finger to her lips.

"Much better." Then he leaned down and kissed her, just a quick, gentle kiss to remind himself of the taste and feel of her mouth beneath his.

Huge mistake. He wanted so much more, but Kevin was screaming his name and tearing across the sand, dragging a towel behind him. Sean's only consolation was the unmistakable shadow of regret in Deanna's eyes, too.

"I don't see why anyone would want to dig for clams," Kevin grumbled. "It's hard work, and they're yucky."

"Not when they're in a big bowl of New England clam chowder," Sean assured him.

Deanna grinned at the pair of them. The clam digging had been Sean's brilliant idea. She was stretched out on a blanket nearby listening to the two of them grumble. The sun was warm against her skin. After only a couple of days, Kevin's hair was turning lighter and his skin was developing a faint tan, except for his nose which had gotten sunburned the first day out. He looked healthy and happy as he knelt on the sand beside Sean, digging haphazardly with his small shovel.

The setting was idyllic, even if being around Sean 24/7 was beginning to take a toll on her nerves. It had been difficult enough to resist him in the city, where she only had to contend with the sight of him in tight T-shirts and snug jeans. Out here, even on the chilliest mornings, he was usually wearing shorts and a T-shirt. More often than not he wore only his bathing suit, exposing more taut, bare skin than she'd been exposed to in years. The temptation to rest her hand against his bronzed chest, to trace the hard muscles in his arms or the six-pack of sculpted muscles on his abdomen was nearly irresistible.

If Sean was having similar difficulty keeping his hands to himself, she wasn't aware of it. He seemed perfectly content jogging along the edge of the water with Kevin running along beside him or engaging in a cutthroat game of cards with Kevin and Deanna in the evening while Hank and Ruby disappeared into town.

This was what marriage to a man like Sean would be like, Deanna realized with a sudden burst of awareness. Slow, quiet days together as a family, accompanied by the edgy thrill of anticipation. Of course, if they were married, there would be an end to the sensual torment. They could spend the entire night making wild, passionate love to each other, satisfying this longing that never quite left her.

Deanna was so shaken by the image that she inadvertently dropped the can of soda in her hand. It spilled over her bare thigh, soaked the blanket and sent her scooting onto the hot sand.

"You okay?" Sean asked, appearing beside her.

She forced a smile. "Just dropped my soda all over myself. It was cold."

"You need to go in the water or you'll be all sticky," he said.

"Not me. The ocean's freezing."

By then Kevin had joined them. "No, it's not, Mom. You'll love it once you get in."

A mischievous grin spread across Sean's face. "Kev, I don't think your mom's going to become a believer unless we prove it to her."

She shot a wary look at him and backed up a step. "Meaning what exactly?"

Before she could react, Sean had scooped her up until she was resting against his bare chest. The sensation of being next to all that sun-warmed skin was so intriguing that for a moment, she completely forgot about his obvious intentions. When she finally remembered, they were already at the ocean's edge.

"Put me down, you idiot," she demanded, trying to wriggle free and escape before he dunked her in the Atlantic. He simply held on more tightly and kept walking.

The icy water skimmed the bottoms of her feet. "It couldn't be any colder if there were ice cubes in here," she squealed. "Sean Devaney, put me down right this instant."

He looked steadily into her eyes. "Now?" he inquired lightly. "You want me to put you down right now?"

Deanna saw the trick, but it was already too late. Sean released her. She hit the water with a splash. It was no more than three feet deep, but she sank into it with a shriek of dismay. It was like stepping under the shower and belatedly realizing that she'd forgotten to turn on the hot water. The shock of cold nearly paralyzed her.

The instant she managed to get on her feet, she brushed her soaking wet hair out of her eyes and faced Sean with a determined look. "You are in so much trouble," she said.

Her indignation was enough to heat her up as she went after him, diving neatly below the surface and aiming directly for his knees. She took him by surprise, managing to knock him off his feet. Satisfied with her sneak attack, she surfaced just as he stood up, sputtering.

"So, that's the way you want to play," he said, a glint in his eyes as he came after her.

Deanna tried to evade his reach, but Sean was quicker. He had her off her feet and in the water before she could plead for mercy. Then Kevin was in the middle of things, splashing them both. When he managed to hit Sean squarely in the face with a handful of water, Deanna saw her chance. She ran for shore.

Sean caught her just before she hit the beach, carried her right back out and sank down in water to his shoulders, still holding her cradled against his chest.

"Ready to concede yet?" he inquired, his gaze locked with hers.

Deanna was aware of every single spot where their bodies were in contact. Given the temperature of the water and the heat they were generating, she was amazed that this part of the Atlantic hadn't turned into a steam bath. She tried to respond to Sean's taunt, but she couldn't seem to form the words, couldn't even think.

Suddenly Sean's eyes darkened as if the heat had finally gotten to him, as well. His hand slipped higher, brushing against the already hard bud of her nipple. Even through her suit the sensation shot fiery heat straight through her. His knowing gaze held hers, daring her to protest or move away.

But Deanna didn't want to move. She wanted that almost innocent caress to last forever, wanted the wild flaring of need to build and build until she was writhing beneath Sean and he was burying himself deep inside her.

Oh, no, she thought with a moan. What was happening to her? She was turning into a bundle of exposed nerves, sensitive to every brush of Sean's fingers across her flesh. If she could react like this with her son just a few feet away and Sean doing practically nothing, what would happen if he truly set out to seduce her?

"We're going to finish this one of these days," he told her quietly, still holding her gaze.

She shuddered at the certainty in his voice. There was little point in denying his claim. They were destined to finish this. They had been for weeks now. Only old fears and uncertainties, which ran deep in both of them, had kept the tide of their wanting in check.

His lips curved. "No argument?"

She solemnly shook her head. "Why waste my breath?"

"Geez, Dee, why not torment me a little more?" he muttered hoarsely. "I thought you'd at least tell me I was crazy to think for one minute that you and I..." His voice trailed off and he glanced toward Kevin who was splashing nearby, safe with his colorful floating device twisted around his waist. "Well, you know."

Deanna smiled at his attempt at discretion. "I know." She rested her hand against his cheek, loving the way the combination of stubble, heat and icy salt water felt against her palm.

Eyes locked with hers, he lowered her slowly to her feet, letting her feel the tension in his body, his unmistakable arousal. With water swirling around them up to their waists, he held her tightly against him, rocking his hips just a little, just enough to make her wish they were out here all alone, under a moonlit sky.

She swallowed hard. "I'd better...I need..."

"What do you need?" he asked, amusement in his eyes.

"Heat," she blurted.

He laughed. "This isn't making you hot enough?"

"Sun," she insisted, refusing to concede. She waved in the general direction of the beach. "I need to get back."

"Because?"

She opted for total honesty. "Because, Sean Devaney, you scare the daylights out of me."

He seemed genuinely shocked by that. "Me? Why?"

"Because you make me feel things, want things, I'd never expected to want again."

He regarded her with a commiserating look. "Tell me about it. This—you and me—it was the last thing I expected."

"Or wanted," she guessed.

"Or wanted," he agreed.

Somehow knowing that he didn't want this—didn't want to want her—hurt more than she'd anticipated it would. Of course he didn't. How many times had he made it plain that commitment was the last thing on his mind? She remembered another man—Frankie— who'd hedged about the future, but she'd been so confident that they could defy the odds. Was she willing to take on another man with doubts?

"It doesn't have to go any further than this," she said stiffly, gathering her pride around her.

He touched a finger to her lips. "I think you and I both know that it's impossible to turn back now."

"Not impossible," she insisted.

He shrugged. "Unlikely, then."

Yes, she thought, refusing to waste her breath arguing. It was definitely unlikely that they could turn back now. If only she could be equally certain just what the future held.

Chapter Twelve

The rest of the week in Cape Cod was pure torment. Sean's desire was a palpable thing—with him whenever he was in a room with Deanna, with him at night when she was in her own bed in a room upstairs. Not even the presence of Ruby and Hank or Kevin's constant chatter could take his mind off Deanna and his insatiable need for her.

He was unable to put a name to it that he could live with. Calling it lust diminished it. Describing it as love terrified him. Better just to acknowledge its existence and not label it at all.

Adding to his level of frustration was the fact that Deanna didn't seem the least bit unnerved by the simmering passion between them. It was as if that moment in the ocean had never happened. She was perpetually cheerful. She didn't seek him out, but neither did she avoid him. She seemed perfectly content with the blasted status quo, while Sean was about to tear his hair out.

He wondered if his brother had gone through any of this when he'd fallen for Maggie. Had Ryan been even half as reluctant as Sean was to make a commitment? Had he struggled with the past, with their parents' inability to stay the course, as Sean seemed to be struggling? He'd have to ask him one of these days.

Right now, though, he was so edgy, he was snapping at everyone except Kevin. He probably would have bitten the boy's head off, as well, but one look at that innocent face with its new freckles and peeling, sunburned nose had him cutting off the sharp words on the tip of his tongue. No child should ever have to pay for the craziness going on in the lives of the adults around him.

Sean could hardly wait to get back to Boston and back to work, even if it was going to be a few more weeks before he'd have Hank back as his partner. In fact, he was so relieved by the prospect of being alone in his apartment, he dropped Deanna, Kevin and Ruby off first with barely a word of goodbye, then headed for Hank's, hoping to escape from there without an interrogation about his sour mood.

He should have known better. It became obvious the minute they were alone that Hank intended to poke and prod the same way Sean had nagged at him during his divorce and was still nagging at him about Ruby.

"You going to tell me what's wrong?" Hank asked when Sean pulled to a stop in front of his place.

"No."

"You and Deanna have a fight?"

"No."

"You and Deanna have sex?"

Sean whirled around and glared at Hank. "You know damn well we didn't."

"Hey, I wasn't watching the two of you every minute. I had my own problems to deal with." He gave a rueful shake of his head. "If this isn't pitiful. The two of us, who have the reputation of being the hottest studs at the station—"

"Speak for yourself," Sean muttered.

"The guys enjoy having their illusions about the two bachelors among them," Hank chided. "The point is, we're supposed to be able to get any woman we want, and neither one of us is getting a damned thing."

Sean sighed. "It's not about sex with me and Deanna," he said. "I don't know exactly what it is about, but it's definitely not the same-old same-old."

Hank's expression turned grim. "Same with me and Ruby. The woman scares me to death. She sees straight through me. The hell of it is, she seems to like me, anyway."

Sean grinned at his apparent astonishment. "Maybe that's because underneath all that flirting and bragging you enjoy, you're a likable guy."

Hank frowned. "But I don't want to get married again, and Ruby's anxious to have kids."

"Has she said that?"

"She doesn't have to. I can read between the lines. She loves taking care of Kevin. She goes all maternal when she talks about him. And you should see her if we happen to run across a baby. The look on her face…" He shook his head. "I can't even begin to describe it. A part of me wants to give her what she wants. Another part…well, you know how I am."

"I know how you are about marriage," Sean agreed. "But children, no. Are you that opposed to having kids? I thought it was in your plans when you and Jackie were together."

"It was—till she made me see that someone risking his life all the time was a bad bet as a dad."

Sean frowned at him. "Hank, you know that's not true. If it were, then firefighting wouldn't be the kind of profession that is just about handed down from generation to generation. Half the guys we work with are the sons of firefighters. And many of them have kids of their own, some of whom will grow up to be firefighters, too."

Hank's expression turned thoughtful. "I never thought of it that way."

"Because you've been too busy trying to prove that Jackie was right to divorce you. Otherwise, it would have hurt too much." He punched Hank in the shoulder. "Face it. The divorce was all about her fears. Some were rational. Some weren't. But getting out of the marriage was the only way she could see to deal with them. Ruby's not Jackie."

"That's for damn sure," Hank said. "The woman's fearless. Last night she suggested we try bungee-jumping as soon as my ankle heals. Said she thought it would be a real high."

Sean had to bite back a laugh. Hank was an intrepid firefighter, but he claimed to be terrified of heights. It was one reason he didn't work at a station with sky-scrapers in the area. "What did you say?"

"Are you kidding me? I told her she was out of her ever-loving mind." He shook his head. "She said she'd go without me."

"Think she will?"

"Probably, just because she knows it will make me crazy," he said with a sigh.

"You are so hooked," Sean said, delighted with this latest turn of events. Hank had enjoyed the heck out of being single, but being married had grounded him, given him a much-needed stability. That was why it had rocked him back on his heels when Jackie had walked out. He'd realized he was losing something important. He just hadn't known how to prevent it, short of giving up his career.

"In fact," Sean taunted, holding a hand to his heart, "I think I hear the faint sound of wedding bells."

Hank swore at him. "Don't laugh, buddy. Seems to me that you're just as bad off as I am."

Now it was Sean's turn to sigh. "You've got that right."

Deanna wasn't sure what to expect after the trip to Cape Cod. A part of her wanted Sean to make good on his promise to haul her off to bed at the first opportunity. A part of her knew that once that happened, she'd no longer be able to deny the feelings he stirred in her. Even that wouldn't be such a problem if it weren't for the unresolved issue of his need to control her life.

Maybe now that he'd seen to it that she had an entire week of rest, it would be a nonissue, she thought hopefully, just in time to look up and spot him strolling into Joey's and heading for a booth in the back. It was nearly 10:00 p.m., two hours later than she was scheduled to work, but Adele had had a headache. She'd gone home early, and Pauline hadn't come in at all. Pauline still hadn't fully rebounded from her bout with the flu, so she'd been taking more time off than usual lately. Joey was relying on Deanna to fill in.

One look at Sean's scowling face told Deanna that maybe she shouldn't have agreed quite so readily to stay. Bracing herself for an argument, she walked over to the booth, pad and pencil poised to take his order.

"You're here late," he said, his tone neutral. "I went by the apartment, but Ruby told me Joey had talked you into working till closing."

"He was in a bind," she said, instantly on the defensive.

Sean scowled. "Joey always seems to be in a bind. Do I need to have a talk with him?"

She slapped her pad down on the table and placed both hands against the edge as she leaned down to scowl straight into Sean's face. "Don't...you...dare."

He actually winced under the intensity of her gaze. "Crossing the line?" he inquired mildly.

"Oh, yeah."

"Come on, Deanna, you know I'm right," he said reasonably. "You're going to wear yourself out."

"I just got back from vacation."

"Which will be wasted if you plunge right back into a back-breaking schedule. And what about Kevin?"

She frowned at him. "Don't use Kevin to try to make me feel guilty. He's getting plenty of attention. In fact, if you were so worried about him, you could have stayed at the apartment and kept him entertained. This is about your need to control me."

He seemed genuinely shocked by the accusation. "Don't be absurd. I don't want to control you."

"That's not how it looks to me."

"I'm worried, dammit. Is that a crime?"

Deanna studied his face and realized he was dead

serious. She sighed and slid into the booth opposite him. "Sean, I'm healthy as a horse. There's no need to worry about me."

"You fainted," he reminded her.

"That was weeks ago," she said, dismissing the incident. "You landed in the hospital the same night. You don't hear me fretting about *you* being back at work."

"It wasn't even three weeks ago," he said. "And it was different for me. I had a couple of minor injuries."

She rolled her eyes at his dismissal of his burns. "And I've had a vacation since then, and you saw to it that I ate everything in sight and got plenty of sleep."

He frowned. "You actually slept?"

"Sure," she said cheerfully, realizing exactly why that annoyed him. "Didn't you?"

"No," he all but growled.

"Sorry."

His gaze swept over her, lingered here and there, then came to rest on her mouth. "We could solve my sleepless nights fairly easily."

She couldn't seem to swallow past the sudden tightness in her throat. "Oh?" It came out as a croak.

"My place. Tonight."

"I thought you were anxious for me to get home to my son," she said.

He grinned. "Not that anxious. He'll be asleep soon, anyway."

"How convenient for you."

"It could be," he agreed. "So? What do you think? My place? I have a chilled bottle of wine. Some cheese and crackers."

The invitation had seduction written all over it. There wasn't a doubt in Deanna's mind that if she went to Sean's, that wine and cheese would still be untouched come morning. A huge part of her was tempted to throw caution to the wind and say yes. Another part held back.

"Another time?" she suggested, not even attempting to hide her regret. "I have an appointment first thing in the morning before work."

His frown slammed back into place. "An appointment at that hour? To do what?"

"I'm looking at an apartment."

"You're leaving Ruby's?"

"It was always a temporary solution. And I really think she'd like to have a little more privacy. Plus, then I wouldn't be the buffer she needs to avoid dealing with her feelings for Hank."

Sean chuckled. "That cuts two ways, you know. You haven't had to decide what to do about me, either."

Just then the one remaining customer beckoned for his check. Deanna stood up, winked at Sean and said, "I wasn't aware you'd given me anything to decide."

She could feel his gaze on her as she gave the man his check, then took his money up to the register. By the time she'd finished, she found Joey sitting in the booth with Sean.

"If he's trying to convince you to work me fewer hours, ignore him," she said as she joined them.

"Actually, I was suggesting he fire you," Sean said, his gaze unrepentant.

Deanna immediately bristled.

"Settle down," Sean advised. "I was only teasing.'' He glanced at Joey. ''See what I mean, though. She's edgy.''

Joey held up his hands. ''I'm not getting in the middle of whatever is going on between you two. You figure it out, let me know. Now get out of here. I need to close up and get home to Paulie.''

Deanna was very aware that Sean's gaze never left her as she took off her apron and grabbed her purse from the cupboard under the register. ''You coming or not?'' she asked as she headed for the door.

''Right behind you,'' he said. Outside, he caught her hand. ''Where are we going?''

''I don't know about you, but I'm going home,'' she said emphatically.

''I'll walk with you,'' he said, falling into step beside her. ''Dee?''

''Yes.''

''Do you have any idea what we're doing?''

''Driving each other crazy?'' she suggested.

''I'm serious.''

''So am I.''

He stopped and drew her around to face him. ''Good crazy or bad crazy?''

She looked deep in his eyes and saw the genuine confusion. It mirrored her own. She lifted her hand to his cheek. ''I'm still trying to figure that part out.''

Sean sighed heavily. ''Let me know when you do, okay?''

Deanna smiled at the plaintive note in his voice. ''Believe me, you'll be at the top of the list. You do the same, okay?''

He nodded. ''Will do. So, what time's your appointment in the morning?''

''Seven-thirty.''

"Mind if I tag along?"

"Why?"

He seemed to be debating the answer. She had a feeling it was because he didn't want to admit that he felt some crazy sense of responsibility for seeing to it that she and Kevin had a decent place to live.

"Curiosity," he said finally.

Deanna nodded. "In that case, I'll see you in the morning."

She was about to go inside when he stopped her. His gaze on her face, he tilted her chin up and touched his lips to hers. Light as a breeze, the kiss was still enough to send a shudder through her.

For a man who worried so darned much about how little sleep she was getting, he certainly didn't seem to mind doing the one thing guaranteed to keep her awake all night.

Sean hated the whole idea of Deanna hunting for a new apartment. He knew just how limited her resources were, even with that settlement from her old landlord. He also knew that despite what she'd said about using some of the cash for the new place, she'd tucked most of the money away in a savings account she didn't intend to touch except in an emergency.

When he arrived in the morning, he discovered he was just part of the entourage going to check out the new apartment.

"Mom and me are looking at a new place to live," Kevin said excitedly. "Once we move, you can come to dinner."

Sean noticed that Ruby didn't look nearly as cheerful as either Kevin or Deanna.

"Sean can come to dinner here," she grumbled,

sending a scowl in Deanna's direction. "I don't know why you're so anxious to move."

"Because we're in your way," Deanna explained patiently.

"You are not. This has been fun." She turned to Kevin. "Hasn't it been fun?"

"Sure," he said, apparently sensing the need not to hurt Ruby's feelings.

Sean gave Ruby a sympathetic look. "You're wasting your breath."

"I know," she admitted.

"If you're going to be a sourpuss through all this, then don't come with us," Deanna told Ruby. "I want objective opinions on this new apartment, not self-serving criticism."

When Sean started to say something, she scowled at him. "That goes for you, too."

"Yes, ma'am," he said, sharing a commiserating look with Ruby. "Where is this place?"

Deanna looked at a piece of paper on which an address had been written. She read it to him. "It's only a few blocks from here."

Sean winced. "And another world," he said. "That area's not that safe."

"Would you stop with the grumbling before we even look," she demanded. "Now, let's go."

Sean sighed and followed along as she and Kevin set out at a brisk pace. Ruby fell into step beside him.

"Can't you stop her?" she asked in a low voice.

"You heard her. She doesn't intend to listen to reason. She'll only hear what she wants to hear. She's in an independent frame of mind this morning."

"No kidding," Ruby muttered bleakly.

"Maybe the place will really be a dive, and she'll

have to admit it's a bad idea," he suggested, even though he knew that unless it was tumbling down, Deanna wasn't going to back out of making this deal. He and Ruby had pretty much backed her into a corner.

When they found the address, Sean was relieved to see that the building was an old brownstone. It wasn't especially well kept, but from the outside at least, it didn't look like a fire hazard. That was something in its favor.

Kevin, however, was regarding it with a doubtful expression. "Mom, it's kinda ugly," he said hesitantly, still clinging to Deanna's hand.

"That's cosmetic," she said. "It doesn't matter, as long as it's clean and the pipes don't leak."

Sean frowned. "You might want to raise your standards just a little to include a lack of drafts. Boston winters can get pretty cold."

She scowled right back at him. "The real estate agent said she'd meet us inside," she said, entering the unsecured foyer and starting to climb the stairs. "The apartment's on the top floor."

"Great," Sean said. "It'll give us a chance to see if the roof leaks."

Ruby barely managed to smother a chuckle as Deanna whirled around to glare at them. "You two want to wait outside?"

"Not a chance," Sean said, staying right on her heels.

The door to one third-floor apartment was open, so they trooped inside. The real estate agent greeted them and began a spiel that would have sold Sean on the place had he not been standing in the middle of the dreary, cramped rooms. She assured them that the water stains were the result of now-corrected leaks. Ditto, the buckling wood floors near the windows. She didn't seem to have an explanation for the grimy state of the ancient kitchen appliances, but Deanna dragged in her new favorite word—cosmetic—to dismiss the problem.

The two bedrooms were tiny, but they did have tall windows that might actually let in a fair amount of light once years of grime were washed away. The bathroom had a sink with rust stains and a claw-footed tub that had lost a good bit of its porcelain glaze.

It was, in Sean's opinion, fairly awful, but Deanna was determined to see it with rose-colored glasses. The price was right and it would be hers.

"I'll take it," she said, even as the rest of them, Kevin included, choked back dismayed protests. She looked at each of them pointedly. "And I don't want to hear one single negative word from any of you."

Sean knew he and Ruby had no one to blame but themselves for kicking Deanna's independent streak into high gear. Nothing short of the roof caving in on their heads before she signed the papers would have stopped her.

The real estate agent beamed as Deanna signed the lease and handed over a check. The agent's day was obviously off to a rip-roaring start, if she could unload this dump before eight o'clock.

Seeing the defiant jut to Deanna's chin as she paid the woman and accepted her copy of the one-year lease, Sean forced a smile. "So, darlin', when do you want us over here to paint?"

She seemed completely flustered by the offer. "I don't expect—"

"Name the time." He'd taken just about as much

of her independence as he could handle for one morning.

"Saturday morning."

He nodded. He might not be able to keep her from moving herself and her son into this dive, but he could make damn sure it was livable before she did.

"What color paint do you want?" he asked.

"I'll get the paint," she said.

His scowl deepened. "What color?"

Apparently she finally realized that she'd pushed him as far as she could push him. "Pale yellow for the living room walls, blue for the bedrooms. White woodwork."

Sean nodded as he jotted it down. "Got it."

"I think I should at least come with you," she said. "In my experience men aren't all that reliable when it comes to picking out paint colors."

"Did you just insult my taste?" he inquired.

"Uh-oh," Ruby said. "Kevin, I think you and I ought to wait outside."

Kevin regarded her blankly. "How come?"

"Because your mother and Sean are about to have a discussion."

The boy's brow knit worriedly. "You mean a fight?"

Sean winked at him. "No big deal. Your mom just doesn't seem to respect my eye for color."

"Huh?"

"Go with Ruby. We'll be down in a minute." After they'd gone, he turned and faced Deanna. "You could accept my help graciously, you know."

"It's not your help I'm worried about. It's the color scheme I'm likely to end up with. I'd feel better if I had a say."

"You feel that way about a lot of things, don't you?"

"Because, in my experience, men aren't that reliable."

"Are we talking paint now, or in general?"

She regarded him with an unflinching look. "In general."

"Dee, have I ever let you down?" he asked, his tone softening.

"No, but—"

"But you haven't given me a chance to let you down, is that what you were going to say?"

"As a matter of fact, yes."

Sean wanted to defend not only his honor but the honor of all men, then decided not to. His father certainly hadn't been that reliable. Maybe everybody generally sucked at relationships. Of course, his brother and Maggie seemed to be doing okay, but there were exceptions to every rule.

Deanna looked at him intently. "You're not arguing."

"No," he said flatly. "I'm not arguing."

That didn't mean he didn't want to kiss her and protect her and swear that he was different. He just didn't have any solid proof that that was so.

Chapter Thirteen

The little set-to over paint at the new apartment was just one more example of Sean trying to control things, Deanna concluded after he'd left with Kevin and she and Ruby had gone on to work at the law office.

"If I don't like the paint he chooses, I'm taking it back," she muttered under her breath.

Ruby regarded her with amusement. "I'm pretty sure he understands that. Did either one of you ever consider the idea of compromise? Did you even suggest meeting him at the home-improvement store on your lunch break?"

"I said I wanted to take care of this myself," Deanna said defensively. "It is my apartment, after all. I'm perfectly capable of selecting paint, brushes and whatever else I need to fix things up. I can also handle whatever work needs to be done. I haven't had anyone to do things for me since I left home."

"Knowing Sean, I imagine he thinks he's just being helpful," Ruby explained quietly. "He's merely offering to take on something that would cut into your little bit of free time."

Deanna tried to see it from Sean's perspective. She was forced to admit that Ruby was probably right. That didn't mean his presumption didn't grate. Once she'd left home, she'd been forced to learn to rely on herself. She'd no longer been able to pick up the phone and hire someone to do whatever needed doing. She'd learned to be plumber, painter and basic mechanic. That necessity had only deepened after her divorce, when money was even tighter.

"If this is going to drive you nuts, call him," Ruby suggested. "Errands are the third best use you can make of a lunch hour after sneaking off with your honey for a quickie or eating something totally decadent. Heck, Sean might even buy you lunch." A grin spread across her face. "Or go with you to pick out a bed."

He'd probably insist on it, Deanna thought irritably, then sighed. Why did she find it so annoying that Sean wanted to help? The answer was easy. It was precisely what she'd alluded to that morning. After Frankie—heck, even after her father's rejection—she didn't trust any man in her life to be reliable. Maybe it was even worse with Sean, because she wanted so badly to be proved wrong in his case.

She settled at her desk, handled the first few incoming calls, took a few messages, then when the phones were quiet, she called Sean.

"I've been thinking," she said quietly. "I can get away from here for an hour at lunchtime. How about if I meet you to pick out the paint?"

"Since you asked so nicely," he said, clearly teasing, "is noon good for you?"

"Perfect."

"I'll pick you up in front of your office."

"It's only a few blocks. We can walk."

"I know you think of me as a big, strong guy, but I am not hauling gallons of paint around. We need the car."

He had her there. "I'll meet you out front at noon," she agreed.

Sean laughed. "See how easy that was?"

"Only because I agreed with you," she retorted.

"That goes without saying. You should consider making it a practice. We'll see how you do when it comes to picking out furniture."

Even as Deanna deliberately hung up on him, she chuckled at his completely unrepentant attitude. She couldn't deny, though, that she was looking forward to the trip to the hardware store as if it were a date for champagne and caviar. Heck, maybe more. Given her family background, she'd long ago discovered that she wasn't really a champagne and caviar kind of woman. That was her mother's domain.

Deanna could just imagine what Patricia Locklear Tindall would have to say if she knew her daughter was going on a date to pick out paint at a neighborhood hardware store. Truthfully, her mother probably wasn't even aware such stores existed, and she surely wouldn't have approved of Deanna dating any man whose idea of a good time was taking her to such a place. Add to that her mother's opinion of any home that hadn't been fully decorated by an interior designer before the move, and Deanna was pretty sure her actions would have her mother's head spinning. And that was even before she discovered that all Deanna's furniture was likely to come from thrift stores.

Sean realized he'd made a mistake in agreeing to let Deanna accompany him when she spread ten different shades of yellow paint chips out on a counter and started pondering them, musing aloud about the advantages of one over the others. As far as he could tell, yellow was yellow. Maybe that was why she'd insisted on coming along.

She finally turned to him, a perplexed expression knitting her brow. "What do you think?"

"This one," he said at once, choosing one at random.

"Really? Don't you think it's a little bright?"

He shrugged. "Looks fine to me, if cheerful's what you want."

"I want cheerful, but not overpowering." She picked up a lighter shade. "How about this one?"

Eager to end the process, he nodded. "Fine. I'll have 'em start mixing it."

Before he could move, she picked up a second paint chip. "Then, again, this one is nice. It's kind of soothing, like warm sunshine."

Sean sighed and waited as a third chip was debated. "Could you at least rule out a couple?" he inquired. "You only have an hour for lunch, and we still have to look at all the blues."

She frowned at him. "This is an important choice, one Kevin and I will have to live with for years and years."

A knot formed in Sean's stomach that had nothing to do with her disinclination to make a decision. It was the "years and years" comment that got to him.

She was making a commitment to paint, for heaven's sake. Why should that bother him?

He answered the question himself. Because it implied that there was going to be no place for him in her life, not for "years and years." She had more faith in the endurance of paint than she did in their relationship.

So what the hell was he supposed to do about it? Was he supposed to ask her to marry him just to keep her from choosing a paint? Of course not. The whole idea was ridiculous, but damned if he wasn't tempted to do just that.

Because the temptation was so real and so disturbing, he fell completely silent and let her struggle on all alone with her debate over the new apartment's color scheme. He wasn't going to be a party to it, no matter how ridiculous that made him feel. It was better than admitting to her just how badly he wanted her to forget all about this whole move and stay with Ruby.

Or move in with him. He was so stunned that such a thought had even crossed his mind, he had to clutch the edge of the counter to steady himself. That notion was even more absurd than marriage. She had a child. She had deeply held values. She wasn't going to move in with him on a whim, not when she was gun-shy about relationships to begin with. Nope, with Deanna it was going to be permanence or nothing.

Sean sighed.

"Sean, what do you think?" she prodded, holding out what were apparently her two final choices.

Since one was right under his nose, while the other was barely in the air, he assumed there was a subliminal message there. "This one," he said reluctantly, pointing to the closest choice.

Her expression brightened. "I think so, too. Now for the blues." A frown puckered her brow. "Or do you think the bedrooms ought to be more neutral, maybe a soft cream color?"

He couldn't do it. He could not debate the virtues of cream over blue, or vice-versa. Instead, he swooped in and kissed her to shut her up. He threw himself into the task, too, feeling the heat that spread through her almost at once, the way her knees buckled, so he practically had to hold her up. When he finally pulled away, she stared at him with dazed eyes.

"What was that for?"

He grinned and shrugged nonchalantly. "Just felt like it."

"We don't have time to go home and do anything about it," she told him.

As if she'd even consider the notion in the first place, he thought, but encouraged by her teasing, he decided to push the point a little more. "We would if you'd finish picking out the paint."

She laughed. "Nice try, but if you think I'm racing out of here to make love with you for the very first time with barely ten minutes to spare, you're completely bonkers."

"Fifteen minutes, if you let me come back and get the paint later," he coaxed.

She patted his cheek. "Not a chance. I want lots and lots of time when we finally make love."

When, not if. He made note of the distinction. Intrigued, he met her gaze. "Just out of curiosity, what do you intend to do with all that time?"

A blush crept into her cheeks. "Use your imagination."

"Sweetheart, the way my imagination's working

overtime, we wouldn't have enough time if we locked ourselves away for a month."

She grinned. "Precisely."

Sean stared at her. The woman had a wicked streak he'd noticed only once before, way back when she'd taunted him with that ice-cream cone. It was now clear that hadn't been an aberration. It was also evident that boredom would certainly never be a problem. Now if he could just shake this overall terror that the thought of marriage and forever instilled in him, he might actually work up the nerve to propose.

In the meantime, he'd just have to settle for getting her to decide on the paint before the store closed for the night.

Deanna was slamming pots and pans around in the kitchen when Ruby got home that night. Ruby stood in the doorway and watched her warily.

"You and Sean have a fight?"

"Nope."

"You did go to pick out paint at lunchtime, right?"

"Yes."

"And?"

"And nothing," Deanna grumbled, then sank onto a chair. "The man is making me crazy. Out of the blue, right there in the middle of the hardware store, he kissed me as if there were no tomorrow."

Ruby stared. "Oh, my. Were you embarrassed?"

"No, not really."

"Mad?" Apparently, curiosity won out over wariness, because Ruby risked coming in and sitting down at the table.

"Only because there wasn't time to finish what he'd started," Deanna admitted. "I have never wanted a man to make love to me so badly in my life. If he'd pushed just a little harder, I would have gone home with him then and there. Instead, he gave up.''

''You mean he took no for an answer,'' Ruby teased. ''Isn't that what a gentleman's supposed to do?''

''Well, of course it is,'' Deanna conceded impatiently. ''But it was annoying just the same. He should have figured out what I really wanted.''

''Men who think they know what a woman wants when she's saying no tend to get themselves in a whole lot of trouble,'' Ruby pointed out. ''I'm sure Sean knows that. I think you'd better be a little more specific if you really want him to make love to you. Maybe set the scene, light some candles, put some flowers on the table, cook him a fabulous meal, kiss him till he can't breathe.''

Deanna sighed at the suggestion. ''Oh, yeah, that's easy for you. You date all the time. You have confidence in yourself. I've been dumped by the only man I ever made love with. Maybe I'm really lousy at sex. Maybe I send out hands-off vibes.''

She knew that wasn't entirely true. She had evidence that Sean wanted her, verbal evidence and solid proof, so to speak. His arousal today—and on other occasions, for that matter—had been unmistakable.

''Oh, please,'' Ruby said. ''Frankie Blackwell was a selfish, inconsiderate rat. He left because he was an irresponsible, immature idiot who thought you were going to be his meal ticket, not because you weren't good in bed. He and Sean Devaney are nothing alike.'' She regarded Deanna intently. ''Is it really about being scared you're not sexy, or is it about the fact that you're terrified because you have feelings for Sean,

the kind of feelings you'd told yourself you would
never have again?''

"I don't have feelings for him, not the way you
mean," Deanna insisted heatedly. "I just want to
make love with him. He's gorgeous. He's sexy. It's
all about lust, nothing more."

Ruby rolled her eyes. "If you were the type to go
in for uncomplicated sex, I'd be the first to tell you to
go for it, but you're not. You're the happily-ever-after
type. You want romance and commitment. You've got
a kid. You're not going to indulge your hormones on
a whim. If you were, you'd have done it long ago.
You've had chances."

"None worth considering," Deanna said defensively. "And I could have uncomplicated sex. I'm not
opposed to it."

"Oh, please," Ruby said dismissively. "How many
times have you told me that you don't even like to
date because it might be confusing for Kevin? Now
you're willing to go to bed with a guy because you're
in lust with him? I don't think so. It's more than that.
You're completely crazy about Sean. You're at least
half in love with him, if not head over heels. Why not
admit it and go from there? Men like Sean Devaney
don't come along every day, you know."

Deanna flatly refused to consider that possibility.
She didn't want to be in love, therefore she wasn't.
Period. "I'm not going to admit to anything, because
you're wrong," she said emphatically.

"I have one word for you—*denial*."

"You don't know what you're talking about,"
Deanna insisted. But the sad truth was, Ruby had
pegged it.

And that was the crux of the problem. Deep down,

buried in a part of her heart she hadn't listened to for years, were feelings she wasn't ready to acknowledge, not aloud, not even to herself. Deep down she knew she wanted more from Sean than sex. A tiny untested part of her wanted the one thing he'd vowed never to do. She wanted to get married, have a family with him and live happily ever after.

Those were the kind of feelings, hopes and dreams that led to heartache. It was far better—safer—to pretend they didn't exist. It was far wiser to accept that there were limits to the relationship. Sean certainly thought there were. His reasons were valid. So were hers.

Deanna might believe with all her heart that Sean was capable of making that kind of commitment to a future, that he was steady and dependable and would never abandon his family the way his father and mother had abandoned him—the way Frankie had abandoned her.

Unfortunately, she wasn't the one who needed to have faith in him. Sean had to have faith in himself. Without that, it didn't matter what she wanted or what she needed. Thinking she could control Sean's emotions—could heal old hurts for him—was a surefire way to get her own heart broken.

She met Ruby's worried gaze and forced a smile. "Stop looking at me like that. I know what I'm talking about."

"You're deluding yourself," Ruby insisted, clearly unconvinced. "Stop making assumptions about what Sean does or doesn't want. Tell him how you really feel. Total honesty is the only way to get what you want."

Deanna regarded her curiously. "Have you told Hank what *you* want?"

The question clearly flustered Ruby. Bright patches of color burned in her cheeks.

"You haven't, have you?" Deanna said triumphantly. "You're pretty good at dishing out advice, but not at following it."

"Two different situations," Ruby said tightly.

"Meaning you have no interest whatsoever in pursuing a future with Hank?" Deanna asked skeptically.

"I didn't say that."

"Well, then? What are you waiting for?"

Ruby's expression turned thoughtful. "I suppose you and I could make a pact. We could vow to jump off this particular bridge together. That way, if we crash land, we can always console each other. What do you think?"

Deanna studied her with a narrowed gaze as she considered this so-called pact Ruby was proposing. "I tell Sean how I feel, and you tell Hank how you feel, is that the deal?"

"Pretty much."

If it would give Ruby the shove she needed to be honest with Hank, Deanna was willing to agree to just about anything. "Okay."

Ruby stared at her with obvious shock. "You'll do it?"

"If you do," Deanna said.

"Okay, then. It's a deal. When?"

"First opportunity. You're seeing Hank tonight, right?"

Ruby swallowed hard. "I said I'd call him if I was free."

Deanna grinned at her. "Then make the call." Her

grin spread. "I guess I won't bother waiting up for you to get home tonight."

"You're being a bit overly optimistic, aren't you?" Ruby grumbled.

"No way. I've seen the way Hank looks at you."

"That doesn't mean he wants any more than a quick roll in the hay. He probably wants it a lot, since I've been keeping him at arm's length all these months."

Deanna regarded her with a pitying look. "Ruby, think about it. If sex were the only thing on Hank's mind, he could have dumped you weeks ago and moved on to someone more willing. He never had any trouble finding playmates in the past, at least not to hear Sean tell it. He's stuck around because you fascinate him. You're unpredictable. You keep him on his toes. Honey, you're a terrific woman. Any man with half a brain would know he's lucky to have you in his life."

Ruby grinned as she stood up and headed out of the kitchen. "Nice pep talk. But if he says yes to going out tonight, I think I'll put on something outrageously sexy, in case you're wrong. What about you? When are you seeing Sean?"

Deanna shrugged. "I'm not sure."

Ruby stopped in her tracks. "Hold it. I'm going out there with my heart on my sleeve, and you're what? Curling up with a good book?"

"A couple of decorating magazines, actually."

"I don't think so," Ruby protested. She handed the phone to Deanna. "Call Sean right this second. Invite him over. I'll run downstairs and see if Kevin can spend the night at Timmy's."

"Timmy's out of town," Deanna said, not even trying to hide her relief at the excuse to put off the promised encounter with Sean. She'd never intended to make good on her end of the deal, anyway.

Ruby frowned at her and came back into the kitchen. She held out her hand. "Give me one of those magazines."

"Why?"

"Because we made a deal to do this together."

Deanna stared at her suspiciously, suddenly aware that Ruby had had no more intention of following through than she had. "You never had any intention of talking to Hank tonight, did you?" she demanded.

Ruby ignored the question and began flipping through the magazine.

"Did you?" Deanna persisted. "It was a trick to get me to talk to Sean."

Ruby peered over the top of the magazine. "Would I try to trick my best friend?"

"In a heartbeat," Deanna said.

"Only if I thought I was acting in her best interests," Ruby retorted.

"That's no excuse."

Ruby laughed. "Is your heart one bit purer? Were you really going to spell things out for Sean, if not tonight, then whenever you do see him?"

"Of course," Deanna said, working hard to maintain a pious expression.

"Yeah, right."

Deanna sighed. "We're quite a pair, aren't we? At this rate, we'll be 102 and still talking about what might have been."

"Now there's a thought that ought to terrify both of us into action," Ruby said.

They exchanged a look, then chorused with heartfelt sincerity, "Tomorrow."

"Soon enough for me," Ruby added.

"Me, too."

In the meantime Deanna had a hunch they both ought to be praying that tomorrow didn't turn out to be too late.

Chapter Fourteen

Sean had already passed the point in his relationship with Deanna when he would normally call it quits. She was getting under his skin. Not a minute went by that he wasn't desperate to kiss her, even more desperate to make love to her. If the reaction had been purely physical, he would have run with it, but it was more than that. Which was why he ought to be giving her a wide berth instead of putting himself smack in the way of temptation by going over to that disgustingly shabby new apartment later this morning.

Then again, how much trouble could he possibly get into while they were painting? As far as he knew, she hadn't picked out any furniture, so there wouldn't be so much as a sofa, much less a bed, to give him any ideas about what he'd prefer to be doing with her to-day. Besides, Hank and Ruby would be there. Kevin would probably be underfoot.

Sean grinned whenever he thought of Kevin with his wise-guy tongue and the expression of total adoration that crept across his face whenever Sean came around. Kevin was a very big part of what was going on between him and Deanna. The boy needed a surrogate dad, and so far Sean hadn't seen any evidence that anyone else was going to step up to the plate and fill in. He tried really hard not to think about what would happen if his relationship with Deanna ended. Or, worse, if she found some other man who was eager to play daddy.

Sean clenched his jaw. That wasn't going to happen, not unless he'd checked the guy out every which way, to be sure he was worthy of the two of them. He was still frowning over that when the doorbell rang. He jerked the door open and found his brother on his doorstep.

Ryan held up his hands and backed up a step. "Hey, whatever it is, I didn't do it."

Sean's scowl deepened. "What the hell are you talking about?"

"The look on your face, the one that says you're looking for someone to punch," Ryan explained. "What's that about?"

Sean couldn't quite manage a smile, but he forced a neutral expression. "Sorry. I was in a bad place."

"I could see that. Want to talk about it?"

"No time. I'm on my way out," he said, hoping to forestall a cross-examination on his mood.

"Then I won't keep you long," Ryan said, ignoring the lack of invitation and stepping inside the apartment. "Where are you off to, anyway?"

Sean studied his brother intently. There was still a certain wariness between them. After so many years apart, it wasn't as if they could just pick up the brotherhood bit where they'd left off as kids. They'd made some progress, but there was still some natural uneasiness over revealing too much, taking too much for granted based on their closeness as kids. A lot of water—a lot of anger—had passed under the bridge since the old days.

Maybe, though, this was the perfect opportunity for another round of long-delayed bonding.

"I'm helping a friend paint an apartment," he told Ryan as he led the way into his cramped kitchen. Since Ryan wasn't going anywhere till he'd said his piece about whatever had brought him by, they might as well be comfortable.

"The coffee's still warm," Sean said, after testing the pot. "Want some?"

"Sure."

Sean poured two cups, handed one to Ryan, then straddled a chair, waiting for his brother to explain what he was doing there. When Ryan remained quiet, Sean found himself filling the silence. "You know," he began, feeling awkward about asking Ryan for anything. "If you've got the time this morning, we could always use another pair of hands. It's no big deal if you can't, but I thought it might be fun to hang out for a while."

"I've got a couple of hours to spare," Ryan said at once, seizing on the invitation as the peace offering it had been intended to be. "Who's the friend?"

"Deanna Blackwell."

Ryan studied him curiously. "Girlfriend?"

Sean debated how to answer that. He supposed that was as close a description as any, but he didn't want to admit to it and then listen to the barrage of questions that was sure to follow. He opted for evasion. "Not exactly," he murmured.

His brother grinned. "Maybe I can help you clarify that. How is she paying you back for recruiting a painting crew?"

"Not like that," Sean protested. "She's just a friend, who happens to be a woman." And whose kisses could melt a steel girder.

"Sure." Ryan's expression was doubtful.

"She is."

"Whatever you say, bro."

Determined to change the subject before Ryan got him to say more than he intended about his relationship with Deanna, Sean asked, "Okay, other than hassling me, what brought you by this morning?"

Ryan seemed to debate whether to let him get away with the obvious ploy, then finally said, "I wanted to let you know I have a lead on Michael."

Sean swallowed hard at the news. The search for the rest of their family was Ryan's idea. Sean was less enthusiastic. Every time he thought of the family he'd lost, he wanted to start breaking things. He hated what his parents had put them through. He tried never to think about them, or about the brothers he hadn't seen since first grade.

But he couldn't deny that since meeting Deanna, he'd been thinking a lot more about the meaning of family. He was a little more open to the possibility of discovering answers to all the questions that had haunted him through the years.

"You know where Michael is?" he asked, his chest tight.

Ryan shook his head. "Not exactly. He's apparently

in the Navy, but when I try to find out where he's stationed, I keep hitting a brick wall.''

Sean suddenly recalled the four-year-old who'd trailed after him and Ryan, eager to do anything they'd let him do just to be around them. The image was so vivid it nearly made his heart stop. Something about that early case of hero worship had stuck with him. It was the last time anyone had looked up to him…at least until he'd become a firefighter. Maybe that need to be somebody's hero was even one of the reasons he'd chosen the dangerous profession in the first place.

Every once in a while when he saw the way Kevin looked at him, it reminded him of the way Michael had once looked up to his two big brothers. Brothers, who, when things got tough, hadn't been able to do anything to make them better. Maybe it hadn't been their doing, but in a way he and Ryan had abandoned Michael, the same way their parents had abandoned all of them.

He sighed and looked up to find Ryan studying him with concern.

''You okay?'' Ryan asked.

''Just thinking about how we let him down,'' he admitted, unable to keep a note of self-loathing out of his voice.

''I know how you feel. I lived with the same guilt for years where both of you were concerned, but Maggie's made me see that we were just kids, too,'' Ryan said. ''There's nothing we could have done differently to change things. When it comes to kids our age, adults are always in charge. We had to go along with what they decided. Now we have to go on from where we are. There's no point in looking back and wishing we'd done things differently.''

"I suppose."

"Hey, you forgave me," Ryan said lightly. "Maybe Michael will forgive both of us."

"Maybe he won't even remember us," Sean said. "Hell, he was only four when we were split up."

Ryan sighed. "Definitely a possibility, but I can't stop looking now. Any idea how we can take this information and use it?"

Sean didn't want any part of the investigation. It was one thing for Ryan to conduct his search, maybe turn up this family member or that one. Then Sean could see them...or not. But the memory of Michael, his lower lip trembling as he was led away by a different set of foster parents, made him want some resolution, too. And one look at Ryan's expression told him he couldn't sit on the sidelines, especially when there might be a way he could help.

"There's a guy in the department whose brother is at the Pentagon. Maybe he'd be willing to do a little digging around for us," Sean conceded reluctantly. "Want me to ask him?"

"That would be great," Ryan said enthusiastically. "I know you have your reservations about all this, but seeing me again hasn't been so awful, has it?"

Sean grinned. "Hardly. How many times have I actually seen you, though? You could start to get on my nerves yet."

"Very funny. Now tell me about this woman we're helping this morning," Ryan coaxed, circling right back to the topic Sean had been hoping to avoid. "How'd you meet?"

Sean told him the story of the fire and all about Kevin. When he was finished there was a broad grin on his brother's face.

"You are so hooked," Ryan declared happily.

"Don't be ridiculous."

"Is she pretty?"

"I suppose."

"Sweet?"

He thought of Deanna's sharp edges and feisty independence, all of it tempered by a surprising naiveté. "Sweet enough, I guess."

"Vulnerable?"

Sean's gaze narrowed. "Yes," he confirmed tightly.

"And she's a struggling single mom?"

"Yes. What's your point?"

"Damsel in distress. Kid desperate for a father. Firefighter with a need to play hero. You do the math."

Sean didn't like the way things were adding up in his brother's head. "Oh, go to hell," he muttered.

His brother grinned. "Not till I get a look at this woman. And before you tell me what a pain in the butt I am, consider this—it could be worse."

"I don't see how."

"Maggie would be all over this," he teased. His face took on an odd expression, and then he met Sean's gaze. "She's got all these nesting urges." He hesitated, then added, "She's pregnant."

Sean studied his brother, trying to gauge how he felt about the news. He didn't know him well enough to read him with any accuracy. "You sound dazed," he said finally. "You are happy about this, aren't you?"

"Happy. Terrified."

"What are you terrified about?" Sean asked, even though he could guess the answer. He opted for being supportive, saying the words he'd want to hear if he were in Ryan's place. "You're going to be a great father. And Maggie's amazing. She'll be a wonderful mother."

"Oh?" Ryan said, his expression skeptical. "Maggie will be a terrific mother, but me as a dad? I don't know. It's not like either you or I had a sterling example set for us."

"Which means you'll try all the harder to avoid making the same mistakes," Sean reassured him, stealing words Deanna had once expressed to him.

"The same way you're trying with this kid? What's his name? Kevin?"

Sean sighed. "Yeah. Something like that."

"A word of caution," Ryan said. "If what you're saying is true, that you're not interested in his mom—not that I believe that for a second—then be careful. Who knows better than the two of us what it feels like to be abandoned? You may not officially be this kid's dad, but if he's come to think of you that way, it could be devastating if you take off."

"Yeah, I know," Sean said. "It's not something I'm likely to forget."

With that thought hanging in the air, they fell silent. Ryan had managed to hit on the one flaw in Sean's plan to keep Deanna at arm's length. He needed to make a decision to stay—or go—before it was too late.

Unfortunately, he knew in his heart it was already too late on all counts. There was no question that he already loved that boy. What was more important, like it or not, he was in love with the kid's mom.

Admitting that to himself was one thing. Acting on it—doing what was right—was entirely another. But there was no question about one thing, he was running out of excuses and out of time.

* * *

Sean had been in an odd mood all day. Deanna glanced at him now and found that he was still wearing the same brooding expression she'd found troubling the second he'd shown up with his brother in tow.

The fact that he hadn't reacted at all to the discovery that she'd already managed to find a few pieces of furniture was especially telling. She'd expected a scathing glance at the sofa, maybe a remark about the bed, but there'd been nothing at all.

Maybe it was because his brother was with him, she concluded. She'd liked Ryan Devaney at once, even when she'd realized that he was subtly sizing her up. In fact, a part of her liked him even more for that. She thought it was great that he was looking out for his kid brother, even after all the years they'd been separated. Though the byplay between them was awkward at times, there was an unmistakable undercurrent of love and a bond that was growing stronger as time went on.

Apparently she'd won Ryan's wholehearted approval, because he'd kissed her cheek when he'd left and whispered, "Hang in there."

She still wasn't entirely certain what that had been about, but she suspected it had something to do with Sean's weird mood. He'd offered to give his brother a lift, but Ryan had turned him down flat, hitching a ride with Hank and Ruby instead.

Kevin was spending the weekend with a friend, so he hadn't been underfoot during the painting, which meant Deanna was now all alone in her new apartment with Sean.

"Thanks for helping today," she said as she gathered up empty pizza boxes and hauled them off to the trash can in the kitchen. "You want a beer or soda or something?"

"Nothing."

She came back into the living room and studied him intently. He was sprawled in an easy chair she'd found in a thrift store the day before. Even with paint spattered on his T-shirt, jeans and even on the tip of his nose and eyelashes, he made quite an enticing picture.

If only there weren't that dark scowl on his face, she thought, barely containing a sigh.

"Okay, that's it," she announced, standing over him, hands on hips. "What's going on with you? You've been acting weird all day."

He seemed vaguely startled that she was calling him on it. He straightened up and looked as if he might claim that everything was just fine, but she cut him off.

"Did something happen before you and Ryan got here?" she demanded. "I know he's been searching for Michael. Has there been some news?"

"He has a lead," he admitted.

Deanna frowned. He'd answered a little too quickly, almost as if he were relieved that she'd asked about the search for his family. "That's good news, right?"

"Yeah, of course it is," he said, though without much enthusiasm. "I'm going to see if a friend in the department can help us follow up on it."

"So it's not that," she concluded. "Come on, Sean. Talk to me. I thought we were friends."

To her shock, his expression turned even darker. "Yeah, that was the plan, all right."

Her heart began to thud dully. She ran a mental movie of everything that had gone on while they were painting, but nothing out of the ordinary struck her. "And something's happened today to change that?" she probed. "Did I do something to upset you?"

The corners of his mouth twitched. "You could say that, though probably not in the way you mean."

"Tell me."

He faced her with an anguished expression. "Okay, since you asked and I don't want to lie to you, here it is. I'm in love with you."

Something that felt a whole lot like heady exhilaration swept through her. Still, she noticed that he didn't look all that happy about the discovery that his feelings ran that deep.

"But?" she asked cautiously.

His gaze held hers. "That's it. I know you aren't interested in having a relationship, and I'm not convinced I'm any good at them, and here I go changing the rules."

Despite his somber tone, she couldn't contain the rush of pure joy. Until she'd heard the words leave his lips, she hadn't realized just how desperately she'd been wanting to hear them. She laughed and launched herself into his arms. "It's about time, Sean Devaney. The wait was getting on my nerves."

He caught her and clasped her to his chest, then leaned back to scan her face. "You're not furious?"

She was almost as stunned by that as he seemed to be, but there it was. She was ecstatic, not angry.

"Furious?" she echoed, not even attempting to disguise her own amazement. "I guess not." To prove it, she kissed him, not pulling back until their breathing was ragged.

A grin tugged at his lips. "Do you have any idea

how much I want to make love to you, Deanna Blackwell?''

She wriggled against him. "As a matter of fact I
think I do," she teased.

"Well?"

"The bed's made. There's nobody around to inter-
rupt. I'd say we have all the time in the world."

Sean's expression turned serious. He reached out
with fingers that trembled slightly and brushed a stray
curl away from her cheek. "You're absolutely certain
this is something you want?"

She touched a finger to his lips. "Not if you intend
to talk it to death."

He laughed. "No more talking?"

"Nope. I think all the important stuff has already
been said."

"Not all of it," he said. "You haven't said how
you feel about me, about us."

"Haven't I? I thought I had," she said, kissing him
thoroughly. "Not clear enough? I love you, Sean Devaney. I never thought I would say that to another
person, but it's true. Not even *I* could be stubborn
enough to go on denying it, when it's staring me in
the face. I love you."

His expression brightened. Before she could guess
what he had in mind, he rose to his feet, still holding
her in his arms, and headed for the freshly painted
bedroom. At the doorway he hesitated.

"Shower first," he said. "Of course, I won't have
any fresh clothes to change into afterward."

Deanna grinned. "I don't think clothes are going to
be a necessity for the rest of the night."

"You going to join me in the shower? Or do you
want to go first?"

Normally she would have wanted to go first, maybe use the time to steady her nerves before she took this next step, but right this moment she couldn't imagine being separated from him even for a second. Despite his claim to love her, there was still a chance he could change his mind about making love. Obviously, he knew, as she did, that they were about to cross a line from which there would be no turning back.

"I'll scrub your back if you'll scrub mine," she said lightly.

His eyes darkened. "Deal," he said, his voice suddenly hoarse.

The bathroom was fairly large, with an old-fashioned claw-footed tub with a showerhead installed above. The tile floor was cool beneath her bare feet. Deanna suddenly shivered, overcome with an attack of jitters.

Sean studied her. "Change your mind?"

"No," she said staunchly. But the transition from fully clothed to buck naked intimidated her.

Sean seemed to guess what was going on in her head. Eyes locked with hers, he reached for the faucets and turned on the water, then faced her and reached for the hem of her T-shirt. Ever so slowly, his gaze never leaving her face, he lifted it over her head.

Then he skimmed his knuckles across her bare skin, avoiding her breasts, on his way to releasing the snap on her cutoff jeans. A leisurely push had the shorts skimming over her hips and sliding down her legs.

Then she was standing before him in bra and panties, watching the desire darken his eyes. He kicked off his sneakers, then shucked his T-shirt and jeans and stood before her in briefs that did nothing to conceal the full state of his arousal. A smile played across his mouth.

"If it would help, we could jump in like this, pretend we're going swimming," he suggested.

One tiny part of Deanna wanted to do just that. In fact, there was something amazingly provocative about imagining how they would look with damp cloth clinging to her curves and the evidence of his desire. Another part of her cried out at being a coward. If this was what she wanted—and it was—then there shouldn't be anything halfway about it. And there shouldn't be any hesitation or embarrassment.

Because she couldn't seem to summon a single word, instead she reached down and unclasped the hook on her bra and let it fall away. Sean sucked in a sharp breath as his gaze fell to her breasts. He reached out and with one finger, slowly circled first one tip, then the other. The gesture was enough to send heat spiraling through her.

Then his hands slipped past the elastic waistband of her panties and slid them off. It was no more than a quick, skimming touch and yet she was shuddering with need somewhere deep inside.

Sean saw her reaction and when she reached for his briefs, he caught her hands. "Something tells me I'd better do this myself if we're actually going to get a shower."

She grinned at the admission that he was as close to the edge as she was. It made her feel something she hadn't felt in a very long time. It made her feel desirable. For too many years now, she'd concentrated on being a mother. She'd forgotten how to be a woman.

Finally undressed, Sean held out his hand and helped her into the tub, then stepped in to face her.

Keeping his gaze focused on hers, he picked up the soap and began to lather it all over her with quick, slippery passes that tried to avoid being provocative. Deanna almost laughed at the concentration knitting his brow. She could have told him all that restraint was wasted. Every place he touched was on fire. Her heart was pounding as if she'd just run a marathon.

"My turn," she said, stealing the soap and using it to work up a creamy lather which she spread slowly across his solid chest. The white foam against bronzed skin made her want to linger there, but there was so much more of him to explore—broad shoulders, muscled legs, a powerful back and tight butt. She could feel his skin heat beneath her touch, felt the tension in his muscles.

"Enough," he whispered, his voice tight.

He turned around and drew her against him, slick skin against slippery heat. His arms loosely circling her waist, he moved slightly until the shower was cascading over them, the water in the old pipes turning cool, but not cold enough to temper the fire burning inside them both.

When they'd been rinsed clean, he shut off the water, reached for a towel and rubbed her skin until it glowed. He barely made a pass with a towel to dry himself before scooping her into his arms and heading for the bedroom.

By then Deanna was restless with wanting, desperate to feel him deep inside her.

Sean apparently felt the same urgency, because he hesitated above her for no more than a heartbeat, gazing deep into her eyes as he slowly entered her, stilled and sighed with obvious contentment.

But being together wasn't enough, not for long.

Sean began to move, the strokes slow and leisurely at first, then deeper and more intense. Deanna's hips rose off the bed to meet him, desperately seeking a release that remained just beyond reach. The rhythm teased and tormented, promising so much but holding back until Deanna was about to scream.

Just then Sean's fingers glided intimately over her, sending shock waves ripping through her. The scream came then, but Sean's mouth covered hers, capturing the sound as he held her tight. Then he was moving again, carrying her beyond where she'd thought she was capable of going, until together they fell off the ends of the earth.

Chapter Fifteen

In Sean's past, the morning after making love with a woman had always meant a hurried escape to safer emotional waters. Even on those rare occasions when he'd lingered for breakfast, he'd been careful to retreat to more neutral turf. He'd done his best not to give confusing signals that might suggest that the night before had been a prelude to forever.

This morning he awoke to the discovery that he was exactly where he wanted to be, where he *intended* to be, for the rest of his life—in bed with Deanna curled next to him, her breath fanning across his bare chest.

Even as he made that mental admission, he waited for the panic to follow. He expected some sort of fight-or-flight instinct to kick in that would have him bolting for the door. Instead, there was...an unbelievable sense of inner peace. Genuine contentment stole through him.

Gazing down at soft-as-satin cheeks still flushed from the last time they'd made love, he felt a smile curving his lips. He could do this. With Deanna he could face the future with the kind of faith that commitment required. He couldn't imagine a time when he wouldn't want to wake up next to her, when he wouldn't want to play ball with Kevin, maybe even hold a baby of their own.

There it was, he thought, as the first hint of anticipated panic crept in at the thought of babies. *That* was the image destined to send a little tremor of fear racing through him. His pulse raced and his stomach knotted.

A baby, for heaven's sake. What was he thinking? What did he know about babies? The last time he'd spent any extended time around babies, he'd been a kid himself. He remembered the twins' homecoming from the hospital, how he and Ryan had held them as if they might break, excited by the prospect of having two more brothers.

Unfortunately, that thrill hadn't lasted. He remembered that the twins had cried more, been more difficult to pacify than Michael. One cranky baby would have been stressful enough. Two caused sleepless nights and frayed tempers. He remembered the strain on his mother's face, the impatient complaints from his father that escalated into shouting matches that often sent him, Ryan and Michael running from the house to hide until the furor was over. He remembered feeling scared and, worse, resentful of the two tiny beings who'd come into their midst and ruined everything.

What the hell was he doing, thinking about having a baby with Deanna or with anyone else? How many times had he wished back then that the twins had never

been born? Now guilt and anguish welled up inside
him at the hateful thoughts he'd once harbored for
those two innocent boys. How could he have been so
selfish? he reproached himself.

With the long-forgotten memories flooding in, he
wondered how he could have buried all of that for so
long. Obviously he'd buried it as deep as the fear that
those childish wishes had been the cause of his parents
taking the twins and leaving.

He wasn't aware that tears were sliding down his
cheeks until he felt Deanna hesitantly touch the damp-
ness, her expression worried.

"Sean, what is it? What's wrong?"

He shoved her hand aside and swiped impatiently
at the telling tears, embarrassed at having been caught
crying. "Nothing," he said brusquely.

She laid her hand over his. "Don't try to tell me
that. I don't believe you."

Her steady look told him she had no intention of
letting him off the hook. He took a deep breath and
forced himself to admit at least part of what had re-
duced him to tears. "I just slammed headfirst into a
slew of old memories."

"Not very pleasant ones, I gather."

He shook his head.

She smoothed her hand over the stubble on his
cheek. "Tell me."

Her tone was gentle, but it was a command. He
knew her well enough to see that. She wasn't going
to rest until he'd spilled his guts to her. What would
she think of him then? Maybe, despite what she'd said
last night, she would be the one who'd flee from the
relationship.

With a sinking sensation in the pit of his stomach,

he began slowly, describing the upheaval the twins' arrival had caused in his family. As he described how the situation had worsened month by month, Deanna nodded, her expression filled with understanding and compassion, not the disgust he'd feared.

"I wanted them to go away," he said, his voice barely above a whisper as he admitted the shameful sentiment.

"Oh, Sean." She didn't seem shocked or appalled, just very sad. "Don't you imagine that's exactly how every sibling feels when a new baby brother or sister comes home from the hospital? You had two brothers thrust on you all at once. Worse, they weren't easy babies."

"But Ryan didn't resent me. Neither of us felt that way about Michael."

"Do you really remember that clearly? You were only two when Michael was born," she reminded him.

"I remember..." he insisted, not ready to let himself off the hook "...as clearly as I remember the tension that began the second Patrick and Daniel came home from the hospital."

Deanna didn't seem entirely convinced, but she said, "You mentioned the twins were difficult babies, and they caused problems between your parents. It was natural for you to be afraid that your world was about to be disrupted. Just look at what happened—your family was torn apart. Maybe that was because of the twins or maybe it was something else, but the bottom line is, your fears had some basis in reality."

"That's no excuse," he said, refusing to let himself off the hook. "They were babies. What kind of man blames a baby for anything?"

She laughed then and pressed a kiss against his lips.

He was so surprised by the reaction, he didn't move, didn't even automatically deepen the kiss as he might have another time.

"Sean, you weren't a man," she reminded him. "You were a six-year-old boy, younger than that when they first came into your life. I'm sure there are plenty of other things you did at that age that you would never consider doing now."

He started to argue, then slowly grasped the wisdom in her words. She was right. He was blaming himself for things that had been far beyond his control. Whatever had happened back then, it was because of decisions the adults had made, not anything he or Ryan or even Michael or the twins had done. The blame, if there was any, belonged with their parents. It had been up to them to cope with the disruptions, to reassure their sons, not to simply take off when things got to be too difficult.

He and Ryan had talked about that before, had agreed on it, but until now he hadn't let himself believe it. Having Deanna, an objective third party, provide a fresh perspective helped more than he'd imagined possible. A sigh of relief shuddered through him as he finally let go of some of the guilt.

Deanna regarded him with surprise. "You really were blaming yourself, weren't you? Have you been doing that all these years?"

"Not consciously," he said. "But somewhere in the back of my mind, I suspect it was always there."

"What made you think about it this morning?"

He started to keep the answer to himself, but she deserved to know where his head was. "I was thinking about babies. Yours and mine."

The expression on her face was priceless—a mix of

shock, wonder and something that looked a whole lot like panic. Sean could relate to that.

But he wasn't scared anymore, because when he looked deep into Deanna's eyes, anything seemed possible.

Deanna didn't want Sean to see just how deeply she'd been affected by his off-the-cuff remark about the two of them having babies. They'd spent one night in each other's arms and he was talking about a family. How could she even think about that? How could he? Wasn't admitting that she loved him a huge enough leap for now?

Because she was so completely disconcerted, she scrambled from his embrace with the excuse that she was starving, that he must be, too. She was dressed in her robe and out the bedroom door before he could blink, much less reach out and haul her back into bed.

Her hands shook as she made the coffee. She had just grabbed the edge of the counter to steady herself when she felt Sean come up behind her, bracing his hands next to hers, trapping her in place.

"Okay," he said quietly. "Your turn. Why did you take off like that?"

"I'm hungry," she insisted.

"Turn around, look me in the eye and tell me food is the only thing on your mind," he said.

She swallowed hard and forced herself to turn around and level a look straight into his eyes. "I want pancakes," she said, managing to keep her voice steady. She was impressed with her acting, if not the blatant lie.

Sean didn't seem quite as taken with her proclamation. "Pancakes? You'd rather have pancakes than me?" he asked lightly.

She laughed despite her tension. "I didn't know you were even on the menu."

"Oh, yeah," he said softly, his mouth covering hers. "Always."

One hand cupped her breast, causing the nipple to bead beneath the soft fabric. Just like that, the panic fell away.

This was Sean. This was the solid, steady man who had befriended her son and protected her, even when she didn't want his protection. Sean would never run out on her the way Frankie had, not after he'd committed to staying. Sean would never take such a commitment lightly. He'd lived through the pain of abandonment, just as she had. If he could take a giant leap of faith into the future, so could she.

Couldn't she? Her heart hammered at the thought.

Then she met his gaze, saw the man who made her pulse race, the man who *loved* her, who loved her enough to face his own fears and move forward.

She shrugged out of the robe, let it slide to the floor as she moved into his waiting arms. Just as he swept her off her feet, she reached out and flipped off the coffeepot. Coffee, pancakes, everything else would have to wait. The future was right in front of her, and she intended to reach for it and hold on tight.

After they'd finally recovered from the most incredible, spontaneous explosion of sex Deanna had ever experienced, she met Sean's gaze and caught the spark of amusement lurking in his eyes.

"What? I'm completely out of breath, and you're laughing at me?"

"Not at you," he insisted, smoothing away her frown. "It just occurred to me that we wasted an entire day painting this place."

She looked around at the bright, cheerful walls. "How can you say that? It's beautiful."

"But you're not going to be living here more than a week or two."

She stared at him. "Excuse me?"

"Isn't it usual for a husband and wife to live under the same roof?"

She went perfectly still. "What are you saying?"

"That I want you to marry me. Today. Tomorrow. As soon as possible."

She stared at him. "A few hours ago we were just friends, and now you want to get married right away?" She couldn't seem to help the incredulity or the panic threading through her voice. "Isn't that a little sudden?"

The earlier talk of babies had been one thing. That had been a sometime-in-the-future sort of discussion. This talk about a wedding had an immediacy that terrified her. Sean had kept her senses spinning all night long. Now he was making her dizzy, moving their relationship along at the speed of light.

He regarded her with understanding. "I know it's scary," he soothed, cupping her face in work-worn hands that were astonishingly gentle, hands that could make her tremble with the slightest caress. "But I love you. You love me. And this isn't sudden. We've been getting to this point since the day we met. If you think about it that way, we've already been courting for months now. And we owe it to Kevin to let him know that what we feel for each other is permanent."

"Let's leave Kevin out of this for the moment."

"How can we?"

"Because this is about us," she protested weakly. "We have to do what's right for us first, or it will be all wrong for Kevin."

"Okay," he said slowly. "Then what are you saying?"

"That I'm still stunned about the fact that we made love."

It was his turn to go still. "Do you regret it?"

How could she? She met his gaze. "Of course not."

"And you do love me, right?"

She nodded.

"And Kevin thinks I'll make an okay dad," he said.

"That's an understatement," Deanna acknowledged.

"Then what's the real problem? Are you going to love me any more if we wait six months to get married? A year?"

Deanna thought about the logic of that. He was right. Her feelings might deepen, as love tended to do with time, but they wouldn't change. Not really. The love she'd finally admitted feeling was as real today as it would be months from now. So, why wait?

"You're that sure?" she asked, studying his face, astonished that all of his doubts could have disappeared overnight.

He regarded her solemnly. "I'm that sure," he confirmed.

The last of her own doubts vanished. Her heart began to sing. She glanced around at the freshly painted apartment. It was lovely, but it was hardly a reason to delay the inevitable. If there was one thing life had taught her, it was to seize happiness when it came around, for herself, for her son. Summer was almost over. A fall wedding could be beautiful.

"October?" she asked tentatively, thinking of the changing leaves that could provide a palette for the wedding.

Sean's expression brightened. "Is that a yes?"

She refused to give in so easily. He needed to understand that he couldn't get his way about everything in their new life. "That's a maybe," she corrected. "October's awfully short notice to pull a wedding together. Maybe *next* October would be better."

"That's more than a year from now," he protested. "What if we get cold feet?"

"I won't," she said with certainty. "Will you?"

"No, but—"

"If what we're feeling is real, it won't hurt to wait."

Sean regarded her with obvious disappointment. "Isn't there anything I can say to persuade you to move things up? How about if I promise to spend every day of my life making you happy, building a family with you that can't be broken?"

She touched a finger to his lips. "I already believe that with all my heart."

Sean sighed. "Then there's nothing I can say?"

"I can't think of anything," she said.

"I guess there is a bright side," he said finally. "At least Hank won't win a few hundred bucks from the guys at the station."

She stared at him blankly. "What does our wedding date have to do with Hank winning a bunch of money?"

Sean hesitated, then shrugged. "Now don't get too upset, but he's got a bet going at the station. He thinks

I don't know about it, but nothing stays secret down there for long. He bet that you and I would wind up married by fall.''

"He what?"

"I told you not to get upset," he scolded. "All the other guys thought it was a sucker bet. Hell, even I thought it was a sucker bet. I'd have put my money on Hank and Ruby getting to the altar a whole lot faster that the two of us." He shook his head in disgust. "I can't believe those two are still dillydallying around. Anybody with two eyes can see they're meant for each other."

Suddenly Deanna saw the humor in the situation. "And if we're not married by fall, *this* fall, Hank loses, right?"

"Exactly."

"Maybe I should re-think this," she said, her expression turning thoughtful. "Winter officially begins December twenty-first." She snuggled just a little closer to this man who'd taught her to dream again. "I know it's not quite as soon as you were thinking, and it's a whole lot sooner than I was planning, but actually I've always thought it would be wonderful to get married on New Year's Eve."

"New Year's Eve," he repeated slowly, his gaze locked with hers. "*This* New Year's Eve?"

"Seems like the perfect time to commit to a fresh start, don't you think?" she asked solemnly, trying to keep a grin from spreading across her face.

For a minute Sean seemed to be absorbing the comment, interpreting it, and then he let out a whoop. Deanna wasn't entirely sure if Sean's delight was at her sneaky way of winning the bet or at his success in getting her to say yes to a very short engagement.

Then his mouth was covering hers, and none of that mattered. In fact, she didn't have any more doubts about anything at all.

Epilogue

Hank was still grumbling about having been cheated out of hundreds of dollars by a few short weeks, but he was decked out in a tuxedo and standing beside Sean as they waited for Ruby and Deanna to walk down the aisle of a church in the neighborhood. They'd considered the same church where Ryan and Maggie had wed, but the reality was that Father Francis's hands were tied, because Deanna was not only divorced, but Protestant.

Once the old priest had heard the whole story, though, he'd said, "That doesn't mean I can't participate in a service held at another church, if that's what you two would like."

Sean had grinned at his clever way of skirting the rules. It was little wonder Ryan and Maggie adored the man.

Now, as the organist began to play, Sean's gaze shot

to the back of the church. Kevin appeared first, wearing a tuxedo that was already wrinkled, a cowlick of hair sticking straight up despite the gel Sean had used to tame it. When he spotted Sean, a grin split his face and he started forward, holding tightly to a pillow bearing the rings as if he'd been entrusted with a priceless piece of fragile crystal. Sean gave him an encouraging wink.

Beside Sean, Hank sucked in a breath as Ruby appeared in a gown of black velvet that clung to every curve and yet managed to have a totally proper and regal look to it. Sean knew that an engagement ring was all but burning a hole in the pocket of Hank's tux. If he was any judge of anything having to do with love, Ruby was bound to say yes. New Year's Eve was going to be a night to remember for all of them.

Then Deanna appeared, framed by splashes of red and white poinsettias, her white satin gown shimmering in the candlelight. Every single thought in Sean's head vanished at his first glimpse of her. She was stunningly beautiful, but there was an unmistakable hint of sadness in her eyes that he suspected only he could see. He also thought he knew the cause.

He held his breath before finally catching a movement just to her side. He heard a whisper, saw her gaze shift and a look of wonder spread across her face. Until that moment Sean hadn't been sure he'd done the right thing. Now he knew he had.

A tall, distinguished-looking man stepped into place beside Deanna and held out his arm. After the slightest hint of hesitation Deanna linked her arm through her father's, and together they walked toward the front of the church.

When they reached Sean's side, her father, his eyes

misty, bent and kissed her, then placed her hand in Sean's. His gaze held Sean's for just a minute and then he moved to take a seat beside a woman who was unashamedly crying in the front row.

Apparently hearing the faint sound, Deanna gasped. Her gaze flew toward her mother, and for an instant Sean thought she was going to burst into tears, too, but she rallied and turned back to face him, her eyes shining.

"Thank you," she whispered. "I know you did this."

"I wanted this wedding to be perfect." Then he leaned closer to whisper, "Don't cry. People will think you don't really want to marry me."

She blinked back the threatening tears and smiled. "Better?"

"Beautiful," he assured her. "The most beautiful bride ever."

The service went by in a blur. Sean spoke the vows he'd written himself, amazed that he didn't stumble even once, not even over the promise of forever. In fact, believing in an eternity rich with love was becoming almost second nature to him.

Deanna's voice was steady and clear as she promised to be steadfast in her love. "Nothing, not sorrow, not crises, will shake the foundation of the family I am committing to give you today. I take you as my husband, my son takes you as his father, from now through all time."

Sean hadn't expected his heart to be so full. He knew as well as anyone that words could be too easily spoken, that promises could just as easily be broken, but his faith in Deanna and this marriage was strong.

Then the minister stepped aside, and Father Francis

rested his hand on theirs. "I ask God to bless this union," he said. "Now and for all time." His mouth curved into a serene smile as he added, "And I now pronounce you husband and wife."

"And son," Kevin chimed in.

The old man grinned. "And son," he added, putting his blessing on the adoption that would officially take place as soon as the papers could be signed.

Sean hoisted Kevin into his arms, then turned to take Deanna's hand for the rush down the aisle and into a future that looked brighter than anything he'd ever imagined.

Deanna still couldn't believe that Sean had somehow managed to convince her parents to be a part of this day. If he'd searched the world's finest stores, he couldn't have found a more perfect wedding gift.

There were still a lot of old wounds that would need time to heal, but this was a start, and she owed it all to a man who had virtually no relationship with his own family. Maybe no one could understand better than Sean how bereft she'd felt all these years. She hadn't understood it herself until she'd looked up into her father's face as he'd joined her for the walk down the aisle. The emotions had almost overwhelmed her.

"You've married a fine man," her father said approvingly, his gaze shifting to the other side of the room where Sean, Ryan and Maggie were huddled together. "He made it clear to me that this was a chance to make things right between us and that if I blew it, I didn't deserve another chance."

"He does tend to be plainspoken," Deanna said, amazed that her strong-willed father had taken such an ultimatum so well. Perhaps he'd been waiting for an excuse to mend fences and Sean had simply given one to him.

Beside Deanna, her mother seemed less impressed. She was gazing around Joey's restaurant with a disdainful lift to her chin. "I just can't imagine what he was thinking, picking a place like this for the wedding reception."

Deanna laughed. "Don't blame Sean. I insisted on it. Joey and Paulie would have been heartbroken if I'd had it anywhere else. Besides, the price was right. They refused to let us pay for a thing."

"We would have—" her mother began, only to have Deanna's father cut her off in midsentence.

"This is what Deanna wanted," he reminded her. "It's her wedding."

Her mother sighed heavily, but a glance in Sean's direction brought a half smile to her lips. "He is a handsome young man."

"Better than that, Mom. He's a good man," Deanna said. "If you'll excuse me, it's been too long since I've let him steal a kiss."

The truth was she was worried about the intense expression on Sean's face as his conversation with Ryan and the obviously pregnant and glowing Maggie went on. Deanna slipped up beside him and pressed a kiss to his cheek. "Everything okay?"

Ryan's expression immediately turned guilty. "Sorry. Sean and I have been discussing family business. It could have waited."

"Don't be silly." She studied her husband's stony expression. "Is this about Michael?"

Sean nodded. "Ryan's located him."

"That's wonderful," she said, but neither brother

seemed to agree with her. She looked at her sister-in-law. "Isn't it?"

"He was injured in the line of duty a week ago," Maggie said. "He's in a hospital in San Diego. He hasn't regained consciousness."

"Then go to him," Deanna said at once. "Tonight, if there's a flight available."

Sean searched her face. "You wouldn't mind?"

"We're not taking an official honeymoon until later, anyway. This is important. You need to go."

Ryan seemed to be waiting for Sean's response. At Sean's nod, a weight seemed to lift off his shoulders. "I'll make the arrangements. You enjoy your party and see to your guests. As soon as I have flight information, I'll find you."

When Ryan and Maggie had gone, Sean stood looking at her as if he couldn't get enough of the sight. "You're remarkable. You know that, don't you?"

"Why? Today you gave me back my old family and started a new one with me. How could I not do anything necessary to see that you get yours back, too?"

"I love you, Deanna Devaney."

"I love you, too." She touched a hand to his cheek. "And when you see your brother again, tell him that we can't wait for him to come home."

* * * * *

Don't miss Michael Devaney's story,

MICHAEL'S DISCOVERY,

*in the third book in
Sherryl Woods's exciting new miniseries,*

THE DEVANEYS,

*which features five brothers
torn apart in childhood,
reunited by love.*

*On sale January 2003 from
Silhouette Special Edition*

And now, turn the page,
for a sneak preview of

ALONG CAME TROUBLE

by Sherryl Woods

On sale in December 2002
from MIRA Books.

1

Tucker stood in the doorway of his bedroom and wondered why in hell there was a woman in his bed.

Unless, of course, he was hallucinating. After the kind of day he'd had, that wasn't out of the question. He blinked hard and looked again. Nope, she was still there. Practically buck naked and gorgeous.

Okay then, he thought, deeply regretting that he hadn't had one last cup of coffee. He rubbed a hand over his face and tried to get his brain to kick in with the kind of quick thinking for which he was known in law enforcement circles. The woman was a reality. That still didn't give him the first clue about what she was doing in his house and, more specifically, in his bed.

He certainly hadn't invited her to share that king-size space, not in years, anyway. He hadn't even known she was there until he'd walked in the house, dead tired from working a double shift and ready for bed himself. If he hadn't flipped on the bedroom lights, he might have crawled in beside her, which wouldn't have been altogether a bad thing under other circumstances.

As it was, he was simply standing here, mouth gaping as if he'd never seen a half-naked woman before…especially this particular woman.

Last he'd heard, Mary Elizabeth Swan had wanted nothing further to do with him. In fact, the last he'd read on the front page of the *Richmond Times-Dispatch,* she was marrying the local delegate to the Virginia House of Delegates. Though that was far from the last occasion on which her name had appeared in print, it was the last time Tucker had permitted himself to read any article that mentioned her. He had to skip quite a bit in the local weekly, to say nothing of entire pages in the feature section of the Richmond paper when the House of Delegates was in session.

It sometimes seemed to him as if Liz, as she preferred to be called these days, was on the board of every cultural institution in the entire state. Her picture—always taken at some fancy shindig requiring designer clothes—leaped out at him at least once a week, reminding him with heart-stopping clarity of just how susceptible he was to any glimpse of that flawless face and tawny mane of hair.

Of course, he sometimes had a hard time reconciling those sophisticated images with the girl he'd fallen for on a schoolyard playground the day she'd pummeled a nine-year-old boy for trying to sneak a peek at her panties while she'd been scrambling up a tree. Mary Elizabeth had been a tomboy back then, and while she'd eventually outgrown tree climbing, she'd never outgrown her go-for-broke enthusiasm for life. Not while she'd been with him, at any rate. She'd looked depressingly sedate in those newspaper pictures, however, so maybe she'd changed, now that she was going on thirty and a force to be reckoned with in Richmond society.

Tucker had finally taken to tossing the feature section aside just to avoid the temptation to sit and stare and brood about what might have been...what *should* have been. What kind of pitiful excuse for a man couldn't get a woman out of his system after six years and a steady diet of gushing reports about the wildly successful man she'd chosen over him?

Lawrence Chandler had high-tech millions and political ambitions. Mary Elizabeth, who'd been born right here in Westmoreland County, came from generations of Virginia blue blood. She'd inherited Swan Ridge, her grandfather's estate overlooking the Potomac. A cynic might have wondered if that stately old house with its manicured lawn and sweeping views hadn't been as much a lure for Chandler as Mary Elizabeth herself. New money seeking old respectability, as it were.

Be that as it may, it was a marriage made in political heaven. If Tucker had heard that once, he'd heard it a hundred times, usually right before people realized they were saying it to the prior man in Mary Elizabeth's life, the one who'd loved her since childhood, the one who'd expected to marry her. Then they'd slink away, looking embarrassed or pitying, which was even worse.

According to all those same reports, Chandler intended to be governor by forty, bypass Congress and head straight for the White House by fifty. Not one single political pundit seemed to doubt him.

But he wasn't likely to pull that off, Tucker concluded, if people discovered that his wife was sleeping just about bare-assed in the bed of a small-town sheriff who had once been her lover.

Tucker might have gloated over this turn of events, but he'd been a sheriff a long time now. Things were seldom what they seemed. He doubted Mary Elizabeth had come crawling back because she realized she'd made a terrible mistake six years ago and wanted to rectify it tonight.

Nope, one glimpse at her pale complexion, at what looked like dried tears on her cheeks and the dark smudges under her eyes, and he concluded that she was here because there was some kind of trouble and for some reason she was desperate enough to turn to him. The thought of the strong woman he'd once known being vulnerable and needy shook him as much as her unexpected presence.

He needed to think about this, and he couldn't do it in the same room with a woman who'd once made his blood roar just by glancing at him with her stunning violet eyes. Mary Elizabeth in a tangle of sheets, with only one of his T-shirts barely covering her, pretty much rendered him incoherent. She always had, and judging from the way his body was reacting right now that hadn't changed.

Tucker retreated to the kitchen and poured himself a stiff drink, thought about it, and made it a double. He had a feeling he was going to need it before the night was over.

$ Saving Money $ Has Never Been This Easy!

Just fill out and send in this form from any October, November and December 2002 books and we will send you a coupon booklet worth a total savings of $20.00 off future purchases of Harlequin and Silhouette books in 2003.

Yes! It's that easy!

Please send this form to:
In the U.S.: Harlequin Books, P.O. Box 9071, Buffalo, NY 14269-9071
In Canada: Harlequin Books, P.O. Box 609, Fort Erie, Ontario L2A 5X3

Allow 4-6 weeks for delivery. Limit one coupon booklet per household. Must be postmarked no later than January 15, 2003.

HARLEQUIN®
Makes any time special®

Silhouette®
Where love comes alive™